MOE JUDY

THE LOFTY SPIRITS

Courtesy to Dr. Adel S. Al Naji who took the picture of the cover around 2002.

THE LOFTY SPIRITS

Moe Judy

In memory, my father HUSSAIN (died 1998), my youngest brother NA'EEM (died 2004), my maternal aunt ZAHRA (died 2015), my mother ZAINAB (died 2017), my paternal uncle HASAN (died 2019); may GOD bless their souls.

PREFACE

To comprehend this story, you may need to understand that the people in this story have accepted polygyny, but not polyandry. Assume that this story occurred some time ago when no technology nor modernism was available.

We do not know whether this story is real, fiction or hybrid when a battle occurred where there was nothing against humanity and war protocols that were not breached. The assailant army atrociously killed men, women, youths, children, and even infants, when, the victims were slain and maimed; namely, all their heads, including the infants were decapitated and used as trophies.

Due to many playing characters and their strange names, people (or maybe beasts as we are not sure) and places' names have been reformed to better understand and classify the side one stands on. The feline names have been used for the protagonist, his family, and his relatives. The bird names have been used to identify the protagonist's factions. The other names have been used to classify the villains.

The story contains prose, narration, poetry, and orations. Each section has been written using a different font for a smooth transition. The prose is written in Times New Roman. The narration is written in Garamond. The poetry is written in *Italic Garamond.* The Orations and Sermons are written in Comic Sans MS.

Also, some footnotes have been provided to elaborate on certain cultural points and values that may not be picked up easily by a foreign reader.

As you read, you may be hit by the number of swearing, cussing, and cursing; but this is how people were, anyway.

I like to thank many people for helping complete this story whether explicitly, like family members and friends, or implicitly.

Please, send your constructive criticism and assessment to the author at Huwaidi@gmail.com.

***WITH** supreme humbleness, inbred charisma, and veneration, surrounded by his disciples and clad in his taffeta and regal attire, Jaguar strolls through the crowded butchery market. Complacently, everyone yields for him to pass. He is a handsome-looking man wearing a beautiful and well-trimmed black beard.*

As he is walking, he notices something that compels him to stop and ponder. A butcher is offering water for a sheep before slaughtering it! Jaguar asks for the reason, and he is told that it is a custom to offer animals water before butchering.

Bewildered in his pose, he bursts into lamentation.

Not knowing what goes on, the people around him fail to appease him. After incessant wailing for a quite long time, he finally faints. One of his partisans brings some water to wake him and then offers a drink. It seems that the partisan already knows how to handle the situation.

People start to wonder. The partisan says that Jaguar runs into this mode whenever he remembers his father who was violently killed after extreme thirst. The inquisitiveness of people starts to grow. Agog to know the complete story, they surround Jaguar for more details.

Jaguar is always eager to tell his father's heartrending story. He sits on the floor guarded by his supporters and encircled by people. Everyone wants to listen to the gripping story. He starts reciting:

Hey sad memory,
if fate has forgotten you,
and savages lost you.
Hey bad reminiscence,
if life has deceived you,
and you disappeared among its rips in causerie,
I will always remember you in recurring hymns,
and yearn for you in traveling songs.

THE LOFTY SPIRITS

Hey poignant recollection,
if years quailed you,
and subjugation spurned over your basils[1]*,*
I would recite you as long as I live,
even if they dumped my mouth with stones.
My heart still warbles with sympathy
although chanting blew up my heart.

My father, Lion, was the son of the great King Panthera Felidae, the greatest king ever. He was a king of similar caliber to David, who killed the tyrant Goliath. He was a leader; mainly like a prophet, messenger, and portent. Lion's mother was Acinonyx and she was the only daughter of another great king. She was so noble and well-known, whom Every man wanted to marry, but her father chose Panthera. Her father said it was an order from supreme authority to wed his only daughter to Panthera because he was the lone worthy man of marrying her.

---

[1] In some cultures, basils are used to adorn brides with. It is a symbol of happiness and good memories.

MOE JUDY

My father, Lion, was supposed to accede to the throne of his father, but treason by Hoar Suidae took over; therefore, Lion had to decamp with his family and patrons to some safe place called Bourg. After Hoar's demise and his son Swine took over, people fed up with the new corrupted system and sent for my father to come for their salvation, and they promised to fight with him against the bibulous and sybarite despot. Lion conferred with some of his family and patrons, who mainly discouraged him from doing so. However, my father, as a hero and never a pusillanimous absconder, was not a person who can succumb easily. He decided to confront the evil, imperturbably. Alas, we lost one of the greatest men in history, ever.

When I was laid up in one of the hottest autumns. Besides me, he took the whole family with him, including women and children. Seventy patrons accompanied him as well. The commander of his few men was my uncle Tiger, the bravest and strongest worrier of his time. Tiger was 34 then, twenty-three years younger than my father. Tiger was from a different wife after my grandmother's demise. Tiger is maternally related to Pig who sided with Swine, the overweening king who bereaved Felidae's posterity from the throne.

Moving slowly on the back of dromedaries and horses, it took my father around two weeks to reach the capital city, Java; however, before arriving there, he wanted to fill up with water and leave for a closer place near Java to arrive in the following morning.

Meanwhile, a person from Java passed by and said: "What brings you here, the son of Panthera?" Lion said: "The Suidaes insulted my kinship, and I was patient. They took my wealth, and I pocketed it. They sought after me by blood, and I hid. I swear that they are killing me, but God will soon disgrace them, exhaustively."

MOE JUDY

In the middle of the day, while traveling, one of Lion's men yelled: "God is great." Lion said: "What for?" The man said: "I saw palm trees."[2]

Lion's men did not believe the man and indicated that those were the tips of spears and horses' ears. Lion confirmed that and asked them to hide in a safe place.

The palm trees happened to be Free-Bird leading a thousand knights. He was sent by Swine Suidae to prevent Lion from retreating to where he came from and getting him arrested in Java. All of this happened during a hot midday.

Lion noticed that Free-Bird and his men are suffering from severe thirst. Therefore, Lion ordered his men to quench the men and sup their horses until the last one. After dousing the men's dehydration, Lion's men filled up some bowls and bear up to the horses and have them quaff for up to five times each.

---

[2] Palm trees meant oasis, and therefore water.

The Lofty Spirits

Al, one of Free-Bird's men, arrived late and he was too weak to drink. As a result, Lion himself quenched the man's thirst.

Then, Lion faced them and said: "I beg God's and your pardon. I did not come here until I received your correspondences that were delivered to me personally by your messengers asking me to come when you alleged that you did not have a leader and wished God to group us over the right path. If you are still holding up to it, testify to your pledges and oaths. Otherwise, let me return to where I came from." Everyone befell silent.

Lion continued: "Hey people if you are devout and know righteousness and its people, you will please God. We are the descendants of Panthera and worthier of custody to this matter than those alleging what is not for them, those who retain adversity and iniquity. If you bear abhorrence and benightedness toward us, and your pronouncement is different from your correspondences, I will leave at once."

Free-Bird said: "I do not know anything about the correspondences you mention."

Then, Lion ordered one of his men to show two portmanteaus full of correspondences.

Free-Bird said: "I am not one of those who wrote to you and have been ordered not to detach myself from you once I see you unless I take you to Swine."

Lion said: "Death is closer than that." Then, he ordered his people to ride their horses and dormitories to head back to Bourg. However, Free-Bird's phalanx prevented them.

Lion said: "May your mother lament you Free-Bird. What do you want from us?"

Free-Bird said: "If someone else told me that, I would not leave cussing his mother whomever he was! I swear to God that I cannot talk about your mother Acinonyx except with the best commendations. However, please take a different route from Java or Bourg until I write to Swine and I hope that I never confront you in my life, again. I remind you that if you fought, you would be killed."

Lion replied: "Are you threatening me by death? Can you dare to kill me? Listen to my reply:

I will proceed.
Death is not ignominy to a chap,
if he truly decides to fight faithfully,
sympathizes with sanctified people himself,
abandons friends destined
to perdition and gainsay felons.
If I live, I will not regret it.
If I die, I will not be twitted.
I cannot sustain living humiliated and coerced.
I dole out myself refuting its abidance,
to meet a colossal army in a fierce war.

When Free-Bird heard this, he gave way. In the meanwhile, Lion was leading his patrons on one side and Free-Bird with his troop on the other side. Then Lion said: "Does anyone know a better way?" Kestrel said: "I do my lord." At that moment, he took the bridle of Lion's she-camel and led the way until they reached the White Province. Subsequently, Lion started his oration that was directed to Free-Bird and his troop:

> O, people. Whoever sees an unjust king, breaking God's laws and oaths, following his whims, treating people unduly, and does not work on changing the situation by hand or tongue is no different from the devil. Alas, these people followed the steps of Satan and averted from the path of God, declared corruption, prevented true laws, allowed the forbidden, and barred the admissible. I came after getting your letters and messengers. You said

you would never betray or turn me in. So, if you fulfill your homage, you will be rightly guided. I am Lion the son of the great king Panthera, blend myself with you, my family with yours, and you have me as an idol. If you break your promise and relinquish your homage, this will not be strange since you have done it before with my precursors. Whoever believed you were a dolt. You stepped over your luck and lost your last chance.

THE two groups were maintaining one path until a messenger came from Java with a letter from Swine to Free-Bird who started reading it until his face turned red. Free-Bird passed it to Lion who read it aloud to his disciples. The content of the letter was: "Once you receive my message, bluster Lion and never let him settle in a place near water or a fort. I have ordered my messenger to escort you and never leave until you do what I demand."

A patron of Lion, Hawk, said: "My lord, fighting these people is much easier than fighting those who are coming next. I feel that we will be facing a colossal army that is going to be too difficult to confront." Lion said: "My ethics prevent me to start a war."

Lion asked Free-Bird to let them go forward a little more. Free-Bird did until they reached Coccus. Then, he prevented Lion and his men to go any further. He said: "This is a good place close to a running river."

THE LOFTY SPIRITS

LION gathered all members of his family including his brothers and other relatives. He looked at them, cried, and said: "O God, we are the only posterity of the great Panthera. We have been dismissed, deported, fazed our rights, and transcended by the Suidaes. O Lord, seize our rights for us and patronize us against the oppressors." Afterward, he faced his men and said:

> People are slaves of life. Religiosity is on the tip of their tongues used whenever it upholds their sustenance. However, if they were closely examined in a calamity, they would instantly depart their piety. As already we are facing what you see, and life has changed, shunned, turned back, nothing is left except an infinitesimal time and ignoble living like an insalubrious

> pasturage. Don't you see that truth is abandoned and speciousness is prevailing? This makes a faithful theist crave for rising to God. I only see death as a glee, and life with tyrants as tedium.

Hawk stood up and said: "We have heard you, Lion. However, if life were eternal and we were immortals, we would prefer to rise with you rather than live."

Eagle continued: "O Lion, the son of Panthera, God favored us by combating under you even if our bodies were to be sliced. Then, your father will be our savior du the judgment day."

Kite said: "Lion, you know that people were not able to absorb the true love of your father or even sustain what he liked for them. There were many hypocrites around him who promised him victory but hid betrayal. They met him sweeter than honey and left him bitterer than colocynth[3]; until he passed away. Today, you are facing the same circumstances. Those who broke their oaths and disowned their homage are only hurting themselves. Take us with you whether going east or west. We swear that we neither pity ourselves nor revolt against meeting God. We are still holding up to our determination and sagacity. We support your patrons and antagonize your enemy."

---

[3]A Mediterranean and African herbaceous vine (Citrullus colocynthis) related to the watermelon; also: its spongy fruit from which a powerful cathartic is prepared. (Courtesy to the online Merriam Webster Dictionary http://www.m-w.com. From now on, definitions will be taken from the same dictionary unless otherwise mentioned.)

FREE-BIRD sent to Swine telling him about the situation. In return, Swine sent a message to Lion: "Hey Lion, I have been told that you have reached Coccus. I swear that I will neither hit the cozy pillow nor eat the luscious bread unless you come surrendering to me or I send you to God."

When Lion read the letter, he threw it away and said: "God never prospers people who bought the creature's satisfaction to disappoint the Creator." Then, the messenger asked Lion for a reply. Lion said: "He should have no reply from me because God's word has entitled him to perdition."

Vocally, the messenger delivered the message to Swine who raged and ordered Hog, who is camping with his four thousand men, to move them to Coccus. Accordingly, Hog would be rewarded to govern a large-opulent and well-irrigated oasis (i.e., Roya). However, Hog asked for a pardon. Therefore, he was threatened with deprivation from anything under his control. Hog asked for some time to think about it. Therefore, he went and asked some of his counselors who chided him. Moreover, his nephew rebuked him by saying: "In the name of God, I adjure to fight against Lion. Then, you will break away your kinship[4] to him. I swear that if you died poor, it would be much better than facing God with Lion's blood." Hog said: "I will not."

During the night on his bed, Hog was contemplating the offer and current situation, and he was heard saying:

O God,
I don't know
how to deal with this ambivalent affair?
My thought is on top of two risks.
Do I leave out the dominion of Roya?
And it's my wish.
Or return back
sinned by Lion's blood?
In killing him,
Hell is waiting, and nothing else.

[4] It is believed that Lion and Hog are related from Hog's mother side.

Moe Judy

However, the tenure of Roya is my delight.
They say that God has created Heaven,
Hell, and handcuffing.
If it were true what they say,
I would expiate in two years.
If it were false,
I would win a great life,
and continuous sway.

THE LOFTY SPIRITS

THE following morning, Hog approached Swine and asked him for a pardon from such a task force. Swine retorted that he would dethrone Hog from his position if he did not do so.

Aspirant, Hog could not disentangle himself from the transgression.

Moe Judy

In Java, Swine was jawboning to people:

> Hey folks, you tested the Suidaes and found them as you wish. This is I, Swine; you have known me for good manners, following the right path, and righteousness to people. I bestow where it should be, and so was my father. After Hoar, his son Swine[5] came and is still generous to the populace. I enriched you with money and augmented your wealth a hundred percent. It is a deed, and I am obliged to commit. Now, I need you to fight my foe, Lion, and I expect incontestable obedience.

---

[5] Meaning himself.

THE LOFTY SPIRITS

After Swine charged the mob against Lion, he declared that belligerence was not an option; it is an order.

In preparation for the battle, Pig led 4,000 men, Barrow led 2,000, Foxy led 4,000, Shoat led 2,000, Duroc led 3,000, Hampshire led 1,000, Berkshire led 3,000, and Yorkshire led 2,000. Then, the total number of men under Hog became 20,000. However, Swine kept sending men until the total turned 30,000.

Moreover, Swine recruited the master of archery, Boar, specifically to target Lion. Boar threw only seven arrows, three of which missed their targets.

Hog lined up his men around the Forbearance River to cut off Lion and his men from water supplies. Therefore, extreme thirst traumatized Lion and his people. Lion sent Sparrow to Hog to ask for a meeting, at night. Then, each of the men (i.e., Lion and Hog), attended the meeting with twenty men from each side. However, Lion asked everyone to withdraw except for his brother Tiger, and my brother,

Leopard. Hog did the same, and only his son and servant remained with him.

Lion said: "Are you planning a war against me? Don’t you fear God Whom you are returning to? You know whose son I am. Couldn't you side with me and leave those, something makes you more devout and closer to God."

Hog replied: "I fear for my house to get bulldozed."

Lion said: "I'll rebuild it for you."

Hog replied: "I am afraid that my hamlet estate will be taken away from me."

Lion said: "I'll replace it with a better one from my own wealth in Bourg." When he got despaired, Lion left saying: "What is with you? May God slay[6] you on your bed very

[6] Historians indicated that Hog was slaughtered on his bed soon after the battle by one of Lion's disciples.

soon and never forgive you on judgment day. Moreover, I hope that you never enjoy eating from Roy's wheat."

Hog hooted: "Barley will be enough for me."

THEN, Hog sent a message to Swine saying: "After all, God has distinguished the revolution, proselyted his word, and brought people back together. Here is Lion, who said that he would return back to Bourg."

Swine became angry and sent back a message saying:

> I did not send you for Lion to leave off, not touch, and make hope for, or excuse him. Moreover, I do not want you to be a mediator for him. Look if he and his men surrender and pledge allegiance to me, then, send them over. If they do not, then attack them not only to kill but also to maim; they deserve more than that. When you kill Lion, I want you to let your horses tread over his chest and back because

> he is tyrannically supercilious. Although I do not see that this is going to hurt after death, it is something I said that I would do if he were killed. If you obey my orders, you will be handsomely rewarded. If you do not, retire and let Pig run the action.

Swine's messenger passed the letter to Pig who read it to Hog who said: "Woe on you, and may God destroy your house. I swear that Lion will never surrender. I see a proud spirit on his forehead."

Pig said: "Tell me, what you are planning to do? Will you obey your master and kill his enemy, or will you give it up to me?"

Hog replied: "No, and no pride for you, but I will take care of Swine's orders. You take care of the infantries."

IN reality, the whole army including Hog, and except for Pig, did not want to kill Lion. He was too good to waste. However, greed and avarice won.

Surrounded by the big army, Lion and his men started to erect more tents. At sunset and as soon as they finished the last one, their water reserves ran out. Lion asked the leader of his patrons, Falcon, to get some water. Falcon took some of his men and approached the river to fill up their canteens. Falcon was a well-known fellow and it was not difficult for him to coax the soldiers to get to the running river. However, they prevented him from filling up the canteens. They told him that he and his men could drink, but they could take no water to Lion. These are Hog's orders.

Additional tents were built to host men and women separately. Falcon asked all the patrons for a meeting. While my father was checking on tents and his people at night, he heard Falcon say: "With the current rate of men, we are dead for sure. You know that we cannot let Lion and his relatives offer themselves for the battle before us. We have to offer ourselves first. We all must defend Lion for the last drop of blood. We cannot let anything bad happen to him while any of us is alive." Everyone seemed to agree with him with vehemence. They all love Lion and are willing to sacrifice themselves for him and his way of living. My father was pleased to hear this coming from his dependable men.

On his way back to his tent, he passed by the family and relatives and heard Tiger preaching to them saying: "Listen Felidae progenies, you very well know the situation around us. We do not want people to say that Lion brought foreigners to protect him, his family, and his relatives. We have to offer ourselves to the battle before the patrons. We all must protect Lion. We all must die with pride."

When Lion reached his tent, my aunt Lioness asked him: "Dear brother; did you examine your men?" He replied, contentedly: "Yes, and only found gallantry and altruism." Lioness is one year younger than Lion and she accompanied him as long as he lived. She asked him to take them back to where they came from. He told her that it was too late. However, he asked for everyone to gather. He told his people that everybody of his patrons can accompany one of his relatives and depart. He indicated that these people want him only and are not interested in others. He did not want to waste his fellows. But they all pointed out that they would be much happier to die with him than live without him.

Everyman went to his tent to prepare his sword for the big mêlée tomorrow. These people were the gist of good people. They were the best of their time. Everyone was preparing his weapons while reading from the holly book. Everyone was happy to support Lion against his enemies even if this meant death.

THE LOFTY SPIRITS

NOT too far from the camp, Pig was screaming: "Where is Tiger? I want to speak with him." Tiger never replied until Lion told him so. Tiger stepped out of the camp and asked Pig about his shouting and reason. Pig said: "You are lucky Tiger. You are a man of protégé. I have gotten the pardon that will save your neck." while handing Tiger a letter from Swine. Tiger took it and threw it into Pig's face saying: "Take your covenant of savory you rabble. You offer me safety while Lion is at stake. What a quid pro quo! Get lost."

I do not really know why these people offered safety to my uncle Tiger. Did they really care for him? Or they dreaded him? I guess both. They all knew that nobody could stand against or face him in a battle. Also, they knew that his maternity tribe would get upset about killing him.

On Thursday night, Pig ordered an anabasis of his army toward Lion who was sitting next to his tent and unsheathing his sword. Lion told Tiger: "Ride instead of me and ask them what they want."

MOE JUDY

Tiger led twenty knights and asked them what they wanted. They replied: "An order from King Swine came to either surrender to accept his dominion or fight."

Tiger left to tell Lion the news; meanwhile, Lion's men stood to preach to Swine's army. Falcon Birdie started to say: "Oh my, the worst people tomorrow, when all face God, are those who killed the offspring of the pious Panthera, these Felidaes who worship God at night and remember Him all the time."

Tamworth replied: "You just vindicate yourself as much as you could."

Hawk replied: "Hey Tamworth, know that God has purified and directed Falcon's soul more than what you can discern. Therefore, I am advising you to fear God. I implore you not to be of help to those astray scoundrels who have already decided to kill the righteous souls."

Tamworth replied: "Hey Hawk, you have never been a supporter of the Felidaes. On the contrary, you had a different opinion before."

Hawk retorted: "Have you become broken to inquire about my previous position to them?! God knows that I had never written or sent a messenger to Lion before. Moreover, I did not promise him support; however, his peregrination had us meet. When I saw him, I remembered Panthera and his opinion and love for Lion. Then I knew that Lion's enemy should never be supported, and I saw to hold up to him, become a member of his party, and protect him with myself after what you have done to Felidaes' rights."

Tiger informed Lion about the position of the adversaries. Lion said to Tiger: "Go back to them and ask for a truce until tomorrow in hope that we pray for, implore, and worship God, as He knows how much I love to pray for and praise Him."

Tiger went back on his mission and reflected on Lion's position. However, Hog was reluctant and asked his followers about it. Cheshire said: "If they were aliens and asked you for that, you would be opted to concur to them."

Essex assented: "Correspond to what they asked you for, and Lion will start the fighting tomorrow"

Hog said: "I swear to God if Lion were to start the combat tomorrow, I would not concur for him tonight." Then he told Lion: "We accept to postpone the battle. If you were to surrender, we would release you to Swine tomorrow; if not, we would not leave you alive."

LION gathered his men at night and said:

> I praise God the best He deserves and thank Him during prosperity and peril. God, I thank you as you honored and taught us. You have provided us with hearing, seeing, and hearts. Moreover, You did not make us infidels. After all, I don't know relatives and companions more loyal or better than mine. May God reward you all!
>
> I guess that our day with those enemies is tomorrow. Therefore, I emancipate you all from my homage. You can all go without blame. The dusk has veiled you so take it as a cover.

Each man of you can take one from my relatives, and you can all disperse in the dark. Leave me alone with the enemy, who only wants me. If Hog seized me, his men would be sidetracked from hounding anyone else.

Everyone refused this offer, and then Tiger said: "Why would we do that; to survive after you? I wish that God would never show us such a time!"

Next, one of the relatives said: "Then, what will people say, and what will we say to them? That we left our master and relatives and did not throw with them an arrow, did not jab a spear, did not hit with a sword and did not know what they did? We swear to God, we do not, but we sacrifice ourselves for you, our money, and our families. We fight with you until we have the same fate as yours. God damns living after you."

The Lofty Spirits

Harrier stood up and said: "Do we unhand you? How will we excuse ourselves from God? I swear that I do not leave you until I break my spear in their chests, hit them with my sword as long as it can stay, and do not leave you even if I do not have a weapon to fight with, then I will hurl them with stones until I die with you."

Shrike said: "I affirm that we do not leave you until God knows that we protect what is left from Panthera. I assert that if I knew that I would be killed, then resurrected, then burned alive and my ashes scattered, and this is done seventy times, I would not leave you until I die before you. How do I not do this, and it is only one death? Afterward, the perpetual honor continues."

Hawk said: "I wish I would die, then be revived, then killed for a thousand times in hope that you, your family, and your relatives survive."

All the patrons spoke similarly. Lion thanked them, and then said: "My people, I get killed tomorrow and so everyone with me, inclusive."

They said: "Thank God to honor us with your support and tribute us for getting killed with you. Don't you, the son of Panthera, wish for us to be at your level?"

Lion thanked them and wished them all the good things.

After hearing that everyone was going to die, my thirteen-year-old cousin, Margay, asked his uncle Lion: "Am I going to be among those who get killed?"

Lion pitied Margay and asked him: "My son, how do you envision death?"

Margay said: "For you uncle, it is sweeter than honey."

Lion said: "Yes; may your uncle sacrifice himself for you. You will die with us after acquiring your valor."

During these incidents, Vireo was told that his son was captured near Roya. Then he said: "I sacrifice him and myself to God. I do not wish for him to get captured and I remain after him."

Lion heard Vireo and said: "May God bless you. You are absolved from my homage. Work on liberating your son."

Vireo replied: "May ferocious predators eat me alive if I abandon you!"

Lion took five of his precious taffetas whose price valued at a thousand gold pieces and passed them to another son of Vireo to pay as ransom to release his brother.

Lion and his pious men spent the night praying and supplicating to God while surrounded by a ruthless enemy.

After one-third of the night, Eagle joked with his companion Robin who replied: "This is not a frivolity night." Eagle replied: "All people know that I am not a person of triviality neither young nor old, but I do that because I am portending whatever we will be facing. I swear that there is nothing between us and heaven except for those contempt people to attack us, and I wish that they did it now."

Falcon came out of his tent laughing. Caracara told him: "This is not a moment of laughing." Falcon replied: "Tell me a better moment of happiness. It is only a few hours until these rascals send us to paradise."

The Lofty Spirits

I was awake on that night while my aunt Lioness was tending me. My father, Lion, secluded himself in his tent for a while with his servant John fixing his sword and Lion was saying:

Oh life, what kind of companion you are?!
How long of rises and sets have you been through?
For a rightful owner to be killed,
and life does not accept alternatives.
Our fate is shaped only by God,
and every mortal is facing my destiny.

He repeated these verses multiple times until I comprehended what he meant; then, I choked with lamentation. My tears came out of my eyes involuntarily, yet I did not say anything but knew that the ordeal is coming soon.

Nevertheless, my aunt is a woman that is full of tenderness and devotion. She could not hold herself. She jumped into my father's tent and said: "Alas, I wish that death took me away. Today, my father Panthera, mother Acinonyx, and brother Ocelot died. You are the surrogate of the dead and elite of the living."

Lion looked at her and said: "Sister, be pious and accept God's wish. Know that creatures of earth die, dwellers of the sky (space) do not survive, and everything dies except for Him. He, Who created everything with His ultimate power and wisdom; then, resurrects people as He wishes when they return. He is One and only One. My father was better than I, and he died. My mother was better than I was, and she died. My brother was superior to me, and he died."

Lioness said: "You oblige yourself to death, which is more troublesome to my heart and harder on my soul."

THE LOFTY SPIRITS

LION went out in the middle of the night to probe the hills and terrain. Kite followed him. Lion asked him why he left. Kite said: "Oh son of Panthera I was worried that you head toward the encampment of the tyrant."

Lion said: "I came out to explore the terrain because I was worried about some ambushes when they attack us." Then, Lion took Kite by hand, and both went back to the camp, saying: "I assert that it is a promise that cannot be broken."

Then he told Kite: "Why don't you pursue your path in between those two hills while it is dark and save yourself."

Kite said: "May my mother bereave me if I do so. Sir, I thank God that He favored me to be your patron. I swear that I do not abandon you unless hell freezes."

Then, Lion ordered his patrons to juxtapose their tents making a U shape and intertwining their ropes together. Lion asked his men to stay within the border of the tents (i.e., inside the U shape so that the tents stay behind them, to their left, and their right).

After erecting the tents properly and sturdily, Lion told his patrons: "Everyone who has a woman in his tent needs to take her to the Birdies away from Lion's campsite."

The brother of Falcon Birdie, Merlin asked why. Lion said: "All my women will be pillaged after I die, and I fear that for your women."

Merlin headed toward his tent. Respectfully, his wife stood for him and smiled at his face. He said: "Don't smile now." However, she said: "I heard the son of Panthera talking to you folks, but at the end, I heard murmurs and mumbles that I could not comprehend."

Merlin said: "This is Lion telling us that whoever has a woman accompanying him needs to take her to our cousins because Lion will be killed tomorrow, and his women will be plundered."

She said: "What are you doing?"

He said: "Get up so I take you to our cousins."

She stood and butted her forehead on the tent's middle pole and said: "You did not treat me justly, Merlin. Will you be happy to see Lioness pillaged and I am safe? Will you be content to see Lioness's veil looted, and mine worn? Will you be pleased to see the earrings of the daughters of Panthera robbed and mine adorning my ears? Will you be happy when your face turns white while mine turns black[7]? No. As you males comfort the men, we females placate the women."

Merlin returned to Lion crying. Lion asked: "What is making you cry?"

Merlin said: "My wife declined anything but standing by all your women."

---

[7] This is a figure of speech meaning that white is good and black is bad, like white angel and black magic. This has nothing to do with any race.

MOE JUDY

Lion said: "May God bless you all."

The Lofty Spirits

ONE of the patrons asked Lion: "Since it is our last night of life, and since it is a night of worship, can you please tell us how your father, Panthera, described God."

Lion recited his father's sermon on this subject:

> Praise is due to God whose worth cannot be described by speakers, whose bounties cannot be counted by calculators, and whose claim (to obedience) cannot be satisfied by those who attempt to do so, whom the height of intellectual courage cannot appreciate, and the diving of understanding cannot reach; He for whose description no limit has been laid down, no eulogy exists, no time is ordained, and no duration is fixed.

He brought forth creation through His Omnipotence, dispersed winds through His Compassion, and made firm the shaking earth with rocks.

The foremost in religion is the acknowledgment of Him, the excellence of acknowledging Him is to testify Him, the faultlessness of testifying Him is to believe in His Oneness, the rightness of believing in His Oneness is to regard Him Pure, and the perfection of His purity is to deny Him attributes because every attribute is a proof that it is different from that to which it is attributed and everything to which something is attributed is different from the attribute.

Thus, whoever attaches attributes to God recognizes His like, and who recognizes His like regards Him two; and who regards Him two recognizes parts for Him; and who recognizes parts for Him mistook Him; and who mistook Him pointed at Him, and who pointed at Him admitted limitations for Him; and who admitted limitations for Him numbered Him.

Whoever said in what He is, held that He is contained; and whoever said on what He is held He is not on

> something else. He is a Being but not through the phenomenon of coming into being. He exists but not from non-existence. He is with everything but not in physical nearness. He is different from everything but not in physical separation. He acts but with the out connotation of movements and instruments. He sees even when there is none to be looked at from among His creation. He is only One, such that there is none with whom He may keep company or whom He may miss in his absence.

Another patron said: "How wonderful his words were. Did he mention how the earth was conditioned?"

Lion said: "Yes, he did briefly in the following sermon:"

He initiated creation most initially and commenced it originally, without undergoing reflection, without making use of any experiment, without innovating any movement, and without experiencing any aspiration of mind. He allotted all things their time, put together their variations gave them their properties, and determined their features knowing them before creating them, realizing fully their limits and confines, and appreciating their propensities and intricacies.

When Almighty created the openings of atmosphere, the expanse of firmament and strata of winds, He flowed into it water whose waves were stormy and whose surges leaped one over the other. He loaded it on dashing wind and breaking typhoons, ordered them to shed it back (as rain), gave the wind control over the vigor of the rain, and acquainted it with its limitations. The wind blew under it while water flowed furiously over it.

Then Almighty created forth wind and made its movement sterile, perpetuated its position, intensified its motion, and spread it far and wide.

Then He ordered the wind to raise deep waters and to intensify the waves of the oceans. So, the wind churned it like the churning of curd and pushed it fiercely into the firmament throwing its front position on the rear and stationary on the flowing till its level was raised and the surface was full of foam. Then Almighty raised the foam onto the open wind and vast firmament and made there from the seven skies and made the lower one as a stationary surge and the upper one as a protective ceiling and a high edifice without any pole to support it or nail to hold it together. Then He decorated them

> with stars and the light of meteors and hung in it the shining sun and effulgent moon under the revolving sky, moving ceiling, and rotating firmament.

A third patron said to Lion: "We heard that your mother said something similar about the creation of things. If you remember it, please let us hear it."

Lion said: "With pleasure:"

> Praise be to God for what He has bestowed with grace, and all gratitude is to God for what He has inspired us with, and all thanks and eulogies be for what He has in advance granted [in the form of varied graces], and the abundant goods that He has bestowed

upon human beings, and all the benefits that He has made, to follow one after the other [for human beings], the amount is beyond the possibility of enumeration, and the extent is limitless, and the eternal nature is beyond human comprehension, and He called upon them [people] to express their gratitude to Him for its continuity and increase, and God caused human beings to praise Him for increasing the abundance of these benefits, and then doubled these benefits for their asking, I bear witness that there is no deity [God] but The Lord, the Only One without any companion; a statement which by its implication, purifies all hearts, beholders' eyes fall short of seeing Him, and describers' imaginations are not able to depict Him, He originated the creatures through His Mighty Power, without any model or pre-planning or any precedence, and caused them to come into being by His might, and created them by His will, not due to any need on God's part of bringing them into being, nor for any benefit to Him by giving them forms, but only in order to establish the proof of His wisdom, and as a proclamation that creatures obey Him, and in order to

> manifest His creative ability and enthrall creation to perform their duty and devotion to Him, and to exalt His invitation; and then God rewarded those obedient to Himself and punished those who rebelled, so as to guard His creation against His chastisement, and to lead them towards His acceptance and pleasure.

A fourth patron said: "Lion, no wonder you folks attract people toward your talks like a magnet. I bet that you inherited these attributes from both parents."

THE whole night was devoted to fixing the armory, worshipping God, and preparing to meet the enemy. Everyone showed great religiosity and piety. All of them were happy as if each were going to meet his dearest lover. Each had a congenital proclivity toward sacrifice. They preeminently were the best patrons known to human history.

Lion and his patrons spent the night like working bees until dawn.

THE LOFTY SPIRITS

IN the morning, Lion gathered his patrons and prayed with them. Then, he lauded God and said: "God has allowed your martyrdom and mine today; therefore, you need to endure and fight to the last drop of blood."

Subsequently, he aligned them for the battle. The patrons were just a little more than seventy people between knights and infantries. He appointed Hawk over the right wing and Falcon to the left. Lion and his relatives stayed in the middle, and he gave the ensign to Tiger.

As far as Hog, he came with more than 30,000 men and aligned them for the battle. He assigned Cheshire to the right, Pig to the left, Tamworth over the knights, Shoat over the infantries, and gave the ensign to his slave Hereford.

Then Hog's army started to enclose and loop around Lion's camp, and they saw fire flaring from a trench behind the camp that was built at night to protect the camp from back attacks. Pig yelled: "Hey Lion. Do you want to taste out the fire before going to hell?"

Lion asked who this was and said: "Was it Pig?"

He was told: "Yes."

Lion replied: "Hey you, son of a herdswoman. You deserve hell more than I do."

Harrier asked for permission from Lion to throw Pig with an arrow, but Lion did not agree to that stating: "Do not throw anything at him. I hate to start the battle."

When Lion glanced at Hog's army which looked like an inundation, he raised his hands to God and said: "God, You are my trust during every peril, hope in every predicament, and to me, You are my reliance and assurance. How many distresses weaken the heart, lessen solutions, convert a friend disloyal, and gloat the enemy that I asked You alone and You instantly resolved them? You are the Master of every boon and the boundary of all desires."

Then he asked for his ride and spoke loudly that most of them heard:

> Oh, people. Listen to what I say and do not hasten until I preach to you about my obligation and apologize for my coming. If you accepted my apology, believed what I say, and judged me justly, you would become happier, and I would not hold you responsible for any commitment.
>
> If you did not accept my apology and did not treat me fairly, then gather your armada and attack me without regret.

When the women heard this, they cried and wept until their voices reached Lion who sent his brother Tiger and son Leopard to appease them as their lamentation would be endless soon.

When the women stopped, he resumed by lauding God and saying things that never heard before, and continued:

> Oh, people. If you get pious, know the truth and give rights to their deservers, you may earn God's gratitude. We are the sons of Panthera and the rightful heir to his reign more than those who made undue; namely, those who have tyrannized and oppressed you. The rightful sovereign rules with the proper doctrine applies

justice, follows the right path, and controls his whims.

Servants of God, get devout and be cautious in this life. If life had been eternal to anyone, it should have been to prophets, messengers, and the best people of the Lord. Nevertheless, God created a life for cessation as its new gets shabby, its fortune fades away, its happiness gets darkled, its house is a mound, and its home is just a shelter. Do good as it is the best to face God with. Get closer to God as you may seek salvation.

People, the Lord created life and made it annihilated and terminal. Its status is variegated. It only fools the stupid. It attracts the wretched. Do not get captivated by this life as it cuts hopeful expectations to those enchanted and disappoints the greedy.

I see you pooling over something that deserves God's anger that obliges Him to avert His mercy away from you. Our Lord is the best, and you folks are the worst. You conceded to Him and believed in Panthera; nevertheless, you marched against his ancestors wanting to kill.

Satan has overtaken your will and made you forget the Magnificent God. Woe on you and whatever you want to do. We all return to God. You people broke your oaths to God which has made Him livid.

Trace back my ancestry and know whom I descend from. Is not the great Panthera my father? Is not the chaste Acinonyx my mother? Is not the righteous Ocelot my brother? Get back to yourselves and admonish your souls. Look if God admitted killing me and attacking my men and family.

Believe what I say because it is the mere truth. I have never attempted lying since I had known that God abhors liars. Lying hurts imposters more than anyone else. If you do not believe me, ask the truthful people around, or even ask Hog himself.

Pig interrupted: "Lion does not know how to worship God and I wonder if he knows what he says."

Falcon replied: "I believe that you do not know how to worship God justly seventy times worse. You claim that Lion does not know what he says. Indeed, God has sealed your heart."

Lion continued: "If you are in doubt of what I say, do you suspect that I am the only living son of Acinonyx? Woe on you. Did I kill any of you? Did I steal? Or did I do anything wrong to you people?"

None replied.

Lion shouted: "Shoat, Hampshire, Essex, and Porker: did not you write to me and said come to pick ripe fruits. Come and you will meet an armada ready to up rise with you."

They lied: "No, we did not."

Lion said: "Oh my God. I swear that you did."

Then, he said: "If you people hate me, let me leave away from you to a safe place." Lion was not a coward or scared, but he hated to have people die for his cause whether supporters or foes.

Essex said: "First, pledge your allegiance to Swine as you will see only what you like, and you will never get hurt."

Lion replied: "No, I do not give in, abject to such people, or escape as slaves do."

Despondent, but not for himself, Lion returned to the camp.

Then, the overwhelming army crawled toward the camp. Out of them, Razorback said three times: "Is Lion there?" The patrons replied: "Yes, he is. What do you want from him?"

Razorback said: "Hey, Lion. Get ready for hell."

Lion replied: "You lied. I go to a Merciful God. Who are you, anyway?"

He said: "I am Razorback."

Lion raised his arms until the whiteness of his armpit appeared and said: "May hell turn out to be Razorback's fate."

Behind the trench that was excavated at night, Razorback went furious, and his horse thrust on him. He lost control and fell, but his foot got entangled in the stirrup. The horse ran, and he lost one of his legs from the hip. The rest of his body was dragged down hitting stones and trees until it was dropped into the fire of the ditch. He burned and died.

Lion kneeled and prostrated for granting his prayer, duly. He raised his voice saying: "God, we are the Felidaes. Break the back of those who oppressed us and stole our rights."

Snout said: "I was the first of the knights who wanted to attack Lion in the hope to get his head and acquire the big prize from Swine; however, when I saw what happened to Razorback, I knew that God respects the Felidaes and grants their wishes; therefore, I left and promised not to fight against Lion if I wanted to keep away from hell."

HAWK could not see and hear these things without reacting. Accordingly, he came up to the army on a horse, which had a long and thick tail, holding his weapon and shouted:

> People of Java, it is a warning for you to get away from hell when advising brothers is a must. Now, we are brothers following the same religion and God if we do not fight each other. Therefore, you deserve our advice. Nevertheless, if we fought, our kinship would be broken, and we would be two different nations.
>
> Hey people. God wants to examine all of us on how we treat the noble Felidaes. We summon you to fight by their side and stay away from Swine,

> the tyrant. You will not reap anything out of him when he gouges out your eyes, amputates your limbs, maims your bodies, crucifies you over trees, and kills you and people like you as he did to the disciples of Panthera.

The army cussed and cursed Hawk. They exalted Swine, prayed for him, and said: "We are not leaving until we kill your man and his patrons, or surrender him and them to Swine."

Hawk continued: "The ancestors of Panthera are worth supporting much more than the son of Hoar. If you do not support them, at least, do not kill them. Leave our man to go wherever he wishes."

Pig threw an arrow at Hawk and said: "Shut up. May God shut your life down. You jaded us with your garrulity."

Hawk said: "I do not talk to you because you are a monster. I do not think that you even know two verses of the holy book. Just await your ignominy on judgment day."

Pig replied: "God is killing you and your man within the hour."

Hawk said: "Do you threaten me with death? I swear that dying with him is much more favorable than immortal life with you!"

Then, Hawk came to the big army raising his voice: "Servants of God. Do not listen to this rough gruff and people of his kin. I swear that God will not absolve people who shed the Felidaes and their patrons' blood."

One of Lion's patrons told Hawk: "Lion asks you to come back and reminds you of the faithful man from among the ancient Egyptians who advised them to leave Moses and his people alone, but they did not even listen. You have done so as well, and you will get the same reaction."

THE LOFTY SPIRITS

WHEN extreme thirst took its toll on Lion and his men, Eagle who was a preacher in Java came to Lion and asked for permission to talk to the people. The permission was granted.

Eagle stood close to the other army and said: "God certainly chose and preferred the Felidaes as they lead to His way. Here is the water of Forbearance that hosts the pigs and dogs of Swine, yet Lion and his men cannot quench their thirst for water that will end up to waste! Is this your reward to the great Panthera?"

They said: "You are talking too much, Eagle. Leave us alone. We assure you that Lion will get much more parched than anyone else on earth."

Eagle said: "People. You threw all the merits of Panthera behind your backs. These are his descendants. Tell us what you want to do with them."

They said: "We need to take them to Swine. Then, he decides."

Eagle said: "Don't you accept for them to go back where they came from? Woe on you people of Java. Did you already forget the messages and letters you send to him under the eyes of God? Woe on you. You invited the Felidaes and you claimed that you would kill yourselves for them. When they came, you submitted them to Swine and deprived them of water. What bad treatment you are offering Panthera and his offspring? What is wrong with you? May God deprive you of water during the judgment day."

Some of them replied: "We do not know what you are saying."

Eagle said: "Thank God who gave me more insight about you folks. God, I acquit from the wrongdoing of these people. God, may You curse them until they meet You angry at them."

Consequently, the people threw him with their arrows, and then he returned to the camp.

LION rode his mare and took a copy of the holy book and put it on top of his head and asked the other army to suspend their clamor, so he could talk, but they refused until he said: "Woe on you. Why do not you listen to me to comprehend what I say? I summon you toward the right path. Whoever listens and follows will win; otherwise, he will perish. You are all mutineers. Your stomachs have already been filled with the bad and your hearts have been sealed. Woe on you. Do not you listen?"

The people blamed each other and agreed to listen to him.

When people gave him the chance to speak, he started his second oration:

> Grief and fie on you people. When bewildered crying for our help and we promptly replied, you unsheathed swords supposed to espouse us. You

fired back flames we ignited together against our common enemy. Devoid of honesty, you have unjustly turned against your supporters and become an iron fist for your enemy. You have no more hope, except the forbidden in life given to you and the degenerate livelihood you are after. We have committed no crime. Woe unto you, for, you hated and left us.

Bewildered, you left us; your swords unsheathed, your hearts at ease, and your choice haphazard. How hastily you flew after life like a fledgling and tottered like moths. Away with you, slaves of whims, deviated troop, negligent of the holy book, deflectors of words, a coalition of sins, discharges of Lucifer, distinguishers of law, killers of the nobles, eradicators of the custodians, bringers of shame, and pesters of the faithful people.

Woe on you. Do you support the Suidaes and desert the Felidaes?

Yes, it is a prolonged perfidy that has evolved with your foundation, joined your branches, implanted your hearts, and coated your chests. You have become the most noxious fruit that distresses viewers yet becomes food to the assailer. May God condemn those who breached their oaths!

Swine[8] has offered two propositions: war or abjectness. How impossible for us to choose servile abjectness as God, Panthera, noble precursors[9], immaculate laps[10], proud noses, honorable souls, and faithful people scorn this for us to favor the

---

[8] Swine comes from a low lineage from both sides as his father was thought to be fatherless (unknown father) and his mother was a harlot.

[9] Paternally, Lion comes from the noblest lineage of brave and honorable men.

[10] Maternally, Lion comes from another noble lineage of women that can never give themselves up to worthless men. Women that are pure and those who can only have children from their husbands (i.e., in no way) they can allow themselves to have any illegitimate relationship whatsoever.

obedience of a sordid group over an honorable death.

I have excused and warned. I will march with my family and relatives although patrons are few, the enemy is countless, and supporters have betrayed us.

Then Lion recited a poem:

If we got vanquished now,
we had always won before.
We might be defeated,
but we could never submit.
It is not cowardice that led to this,
but our destiny.
If death is delayed for some,
it for sure comes to others.
Death reaps the bravest

as it had to previous nations.
If kings were immortals,
we would be as well.
If noble people lingered,
we would for sure remain.
Tell the gloaters to wake up
as they will encounter our fate.

Then, he continued his oration:

I affirm that you will not last after this for long until life circles you as a quern does. This is a promise; therefore, revise your intentions lest they bring you melancholy. Come back to me and do not wait because I have left my trust to the Lord, my God, and yours. There is no soul that He is not taking care of. My God is the ultimate justice.

Afterward, Lion raised his hand to God and continued:

O God, deprive these people of the rain. Punish them with years like those of Joseph[11]. God, have Osprey[12] avenge them. Have them swallow his bitter doses. Have him kill them, one by one, a kill by a kill, and a hit by another. Have him revenge for me and my folks as these people deceived, lied, and betrayed us. You are our God. We believe in and trust You. We submit to

---

[11] The son of Jacob (Israel) as seven bad years took over Egypt.

[12] One of Lion's patrons who was arrested and put in prison during this incident.

You, and our providence comes always back to You.

THE LOFTY SPIRITS

SUBSEQUENTLY, Lion called for Hog who hated to meet Lion. When Hog came, Lion told him: "Hog, do you aver to kill me, and then believe that Swine appoints you to rule Roya? I avow that you will not be delighted to do so. It is a pledge. Do whatever you want to do, but you will never ever get joyful after me neither in nor beyond life. I foresee[13] your head on top of a reed thrown at by the kids of Java in turns." Hog irately averted his face but did not say anything.

[13] History confirms this prophecy.

MOE JUDY

WHEN he heard Lion and realized that the army persisted in killing him, Free-Bird came to Hog and asked him: "Are you really fighting against Lion?"

Hog said: "Yes, with a battle that at least will reap out heads and cut off hands."

Free-Bird said: "Even after seeing and hearing his valor, nobility, honesty, and meritocracy?"

Hog replied: "I would agree if it were up to me, but it is Swine's wish and decision."

Free-Bird left and stood with the rout. Besides him was Snout. Free-Bird asked him: "Did you let your mare drink today?”

Snout said: "No."

Free-Bird asked: "Would you like for her to drink?"

Snout realized that Free-Bird wanted to retire, and he hated to be witnessed.

THE LOFTY SPIRITS

Gradually, Free-Bird came closer to Lion's camp. He was spotted by Warty who said: "Are you charging?" Free-Bird did not say anything but was trembling. Warty rebuked such behavior from Free-Bird and said: "Your situation is dubious. I have not seen people like you in such circumstances in your current condition. If I had been asked who the bravest man in Java was, I would not have missed you. What is this that I see from you now?" Free-Bird replied: "I am choosing between heaven and hell. In no way, I would choose something other than heaven even if I were burned."

Free-Bird rode his horse toward Lion's camp inverting his spear, reversing his shield, and bowing his head, as he was the cause for Lion and his followers to face such fate. He was vocalizing: "God, I turn to You in repentance. Please, exonerate me as I frightened the hearts of these noble people and descendants of Panthera."

When Free-Bird approached Lion's tent, he raised his voice saying: "The son of Panthera, may I be sacrificed for your sake as I prevented you from going back and forced you to this wicked place. I never thought that those people would turn their backs on your propositions. If I had known this before, I would not have done so. I repent to God and want to be with you until I die for you. Do you see that God will absolve my awful conduct?"

Lion replied: "Yes, God will. Come down."

Free-Bird said: "I am better of a knight than an infantry. I compact them on my horse until I am forced to come down. Then, this would be the last of me."

Lion said: "May God bless you. Do whatever you find fit."

FREE-BIRD proceeded toward Swine army to preach and reproach them saying:

> People of Java, you are truly a suitable example of imprudence.
>
> You summoned this great man of God until he came, and you want to detain him! You claimed that you would kill yourselves for him, and then you beset to kill him! You apprehended his soul and latched his throat. Moreover, you surrounded him to thwart him to go anywhere else. He became like a prisoner of war at your hands. He can neither do good to himself nor prevent bad. You banned him, women, kids, his family, and relatives from the running water of

> Forbearance whose water is used by pigs, dogs, and snakes. Lion and his people are almost dying from thirst.
>
> Woe on you people for treating Panthera's offspring this way. May God prevent you from water during the day of extreme thirst[14].

Free-Bird was attacked by arrows. He returned and shielded Lion.

---

[14] The judgment day is believed to be the day of extreme thirst.

The Lofty Spirits

Hog advanced toward Lion's camp and threw an arrow and said to his army: "You are my witnesses to Swine that I was the first to throw."

Then his men threw their arrows that came like pouring rain, which in turn hit everyone in Lion's camp. Lion said: "May God bless you all. Get ready for an indispensable fate. These arrows are the messengers of the enemy."

FREE-BIRD looked at Lion and said: "I was the first to go against you. Please, allow me to be the first to die for you in the hope to shake Panthera's hand during the judgment day."

Lion permitted him first. Then, he charged against Hog's army while improvising:

I am Free-Bird and the shelter for guests.
I chop your necks with my sword,
for the sake of the best man on earth.
I knock you down without regrets.

He continued his bravery until his horse was hamstrung. Then, he came down fighting on foot saying:

I decided not to die,
until I kill
striking them with my sword
punching hard hits.
I am neither scared

nor affected.
I am neither incapable
nor distorted.

He fought a fierce battle until he killed more than forty people. He was attacking along with Hawk. If one of them charged and penetrated the enemy, the other came for rescue. Then, many people surrounded Free-Bird until they beat him. Accordingly, Lion's men carried, tremendously-bleeding, Free-Bird to the camp and put him before Lion who started to clean the blood and sand off his face while saying: "Well done Free-Bird. You are free in life as your mother dubbed you and a happy afterlife."

When Free-Bird passed away, one of Lion's men elegized him:

What an excellent free man Free-Bird is!
He endures during wars.
What an admirable sacrifice for Lion.

MOE JUDY

Jay was originally one of Swine's men; however, he disapproved of the way Lion was treated, he left Swine and joined Lion and started to fight for Lion saying:

I am Jay and my father was the traveler,
braver than a charging lion.
O God, I am a patron of Lion,
and not for Swine, I am dying.

Jay knelt in front of Lion and threw a hundred arrows. Every time Jay threw, Lion prayed for him: "God makes his throws pertinent now, and heaven his home, then." Jay killed five people of the enemy and he was the first to be killed from Lion's men.

THE LOFTY SPIRITS

THE two camps entangled together and fought for an hour until most people of Lion's camp got butchered and killed. Lion held his beard and said: "God's anger amplified over people who consented to kill the son of Panthera. O God, I will never submit to their wishes until I meet you dyeing my beard with my blood." Then, Lion shouted: "Is there anyone there who can succor us? Is there anyone there to expel the beasts away from our women and kids?"

Two of Swine's slaves, Snake and Serpent, asked who could duel with them. Falcon and Eagle jumped to combat them, but Lion did not permit them.

Crane, who came from Java the previous night, stood up and asked for permission from Lion to fight Snake and Serpent. Crane was tall and had wide shoulders. He also was honorable among his tribe and a tested-brave man. Lion looked at him and said: "I believe that he is the right fit to fight those two." Lion permitted him.

MOE JUDY

When he revealed himself to the encounter, Snake asked: "Who are you?"

Crane introduced himself, but Snake said: "I do not know you. I want to face Hawk, Falcon, or Eagle."

Crane said: "You are a hypocrite. You want to combat someone of less caliber than you. Know that every one of Lion's men is much superior to you."

Crane charged against Snake. While Crane was busy, Serpent attacked him; thus, Lion's men shouted: "Lookout for the slave," but Crane was busy. Accordingly, Serpent hit Crane who received it with his left hand which caused his fingers to get cut off. Then, Crane faced Serpent and killed him after killing Snake.

Crane went back to the battlefield and killed two other men until numerous people attacked him and severed his leg. Subsequently, he was taken as a prisoner of war, and he was viciously terminated.

THE LOFTY SPIRITS

BUNTING stepped forward to the battle. Lion told him: "Go. We are meeting within the hour." His servant followed him along with Bushtit and Cardinal. The four of them charged against the enemy who cut them off from their camp when Lion sent his brother Tiger to help them out as they were all injured. Coming back, the four were attacked by the enemy and all were killed in the same spot.

When the patrons realized that there were only a few of them left and many of them were killed, they started to go by twos, threes, and fours asking for Lion's permission to protect him and his family. Each person in the group was protecting the back of another member.

During this, two of his patrons who happened to be cousins and brothers from the same mother, Chickadee, and Coot, came to get Lion's permission for the battle. He permitted them. They fought an honorable fight, and both died.

LION shouted: "Is there anyone there who can succor us? Is there anyone there to expel the beasts away from our women and kids?" When the women and kids heard him, they bawled. With Swine's army, Flicker and his brother Grouse heard Lion's sermonizing and the women and kids weeping. They took their swords and started to assail Swine's army killing several people and injuring several men as well until they got killed together.

THE LOFTY SPIRITS

AFTER a few men remained with Lion and their shortage became noticeable, they started to duel with the enemy one by one. This way, they killed many soldiers of Swine's army, something that Cheshire did not like very much, and shouted: "Do you know whom you are fighting; fools? These are the best knights of the nation. They are people of sagacity. They are death-defying. Although they are few, they can kill any dupe who wants to combat them. You idiots, if you only threw stones at them, you would cease them all."

Hog replied: "That is true, Cheshire. Warn the army not to duel with them anymore, and if our people do that, they will all finish." Cheshire got closer to Lion's camp and said to Swine's army: "People of Java. Stay obedient. Never have a second thought of killing the rebels and recants." Lion said: "Cheshire, do you goad the people against us? Are we the recants, and you are authentic? I swear that you know who the recanter is and who deserves hell."

CHESHIRE took his men and attacked Lion's camp from the right, but Lion's men were securely steadfast as they knelt and pointed out their spears that thwarted horses and knights who retreated, during which, the patrons threw their arrows that killed and injured many. Cheshire changed his tactics and came from Forbearance and had a fierce fight with the patrons that included Harrier, Kinglet, and Lark. The dust blurred everything. As soon as it cleared, Harrier was found at his last gasp. Lion walked to him with Falcon. Lion said: "May God bless you, Harrier." Falcon got closer and said: "It is really hard for me to watch you like this; however, heaven will be your destiny."

Harrier replied in a weak-low voice: "Thank you."

Falcon said: "If I did not know that I would accompany you soon, I would ask you what you want to bequeath."

Harrier pointed his finger toward Lion and said: "Him. Take care of him. No harm shall threaten him as long as you are alive. Fight for him until you die."

Falcon: "I will surely do." Then, Harrier passed away.

Swine's army got happy and some of them said: "We killed Harrier." Shoat said: "May your mothers bereave you; clowns. I see that you kill and abase yourselves by your own hands. Do you get joyful by killing Harrier? I had accompanied him before and seen how brave and generous he was. He is one to cry for, instead."

PIG took some of his men to attack Lion's pavilion. He gored the garment and said: "Give me a torch to burn down the canopy of the oppressors over its residents." The women cried, took the children, and left the pavilion. Lion yelled: "Hey Pig, do you want to burn down my house over my family? May God burn you in hell."

Shoat told Pig: "Are you petrifying women and kids? I swear that I have not seen worse than your talk and attitude."

Subsequently, Hawk took ten of Lion's men and charged against Pig and his thugs that forced them to retreat after killing Gila from Pig's ruffians.

A chief in his tribe, Martin stood to fight for Lion. He fought like an intrepid lion and endured like a patient camel until he fell among the dead patrons. He was thought to be dead because he was not moving for a long time until he heard: "Lion was killed." After that, he endured, stood up, took his knife from his scuff, and started to fight. He was killed. He was the last to be finished from among Lion's camp.

PHEASANT noticed zenith and informed Lion about that indicating it was time for the midday prayer. He told Lion: "My soul is a sacrifice to yours. I see the enemy coming closer to your camp. I swear that you will not be killed until I die for you first. I wish to meet God after praying with you, though."

Lion looked at the sky and said: "You remembered the prayer. May God make you one of the pious prayers! Yes, this is time. Ask the army to stop until we pray." The remaining men of Lion asked Swine's army to stop for the coming prayer.

One of Hog's men, Foxy, said: "It will not be accepted from you."

Falcon replied: "You claimed that it would not be accepted by the Felidaes and accepted it from a sot like you!"

Incensed, Foxy plunged against Falcon who smacked the face of Foxy's mare that pranced, and caused Foxy to fall, but his men rescued him, immediately.

Moe Judy

ALTHOUGH he was seventy-five, Falcon was fighting like a youthful knight. Alone, he killed sixty-two men. Finally, and after being surrounded by too many brutes, Falcon was hit on his head by Glutton, and gored by Lizard's spear; only then, Falcon fell. He wanted to get up, but he was hit by Foxy on his head which caused him to fall on his face. Glutton debarked and beheaded Falcon. Lion saw this and lamented: "I sacrifice myself and men to God." Lion repeated for some time: "We are all from God, and we will all return to Him."

THE LOFTY SPIRITS

LION was performing his prayers with the few remaining men. Hawk and Shrike stood in front of Lion to protect him from arrows.

Every time an arrow came, Shrike confronted it with his chest and face until he was enervated and fell saying: "O God, condemn these hooligans as You did to previous sordid nations. God, please deliver my regards to Panthera and inform him about the pain and injuries that I encountered. I just wanted Your requital toward standing for the Felidaes." Before his last breath left him, he asked Lion: "Did I pay full dues to you?" Lion said: "Yes, you did do, and you will be in front of me in heaven." When he died, Shrike had thirteen arrows planted in his body along with many hits and jabs.

When Lion finished his prayers, he told his patrons: "O noble people. There is heaven opening its gates for you to see its river and ripe fruits. There is Panthera and the martyrs who died for God's sake waiting merrily for you.

Defend the true faith of God and protect the women and children of Panthera."

They all said: "Our souls are sacrifices for yours. Our blood shields yours. We swear that no harm will be done to you as long as we breathe."

Hog ordered Cheshire to take some of his men and throw as many arrows as they could at Lion's men. He also ordered them to slay their horses as well. The battle started to heat up again. As there were not many men left, only one or two would go to the battlefield leaving Lion and saying: "Peace be upon you the son of Panthera." Lion replied: "And peace may be on you, too. Go and we will soon follow."

A cousin of Hawk, Phoebe, was also one of the patrons who fought and got killed. Another patron was also Puffin.

MOE JUDY

HAWK is of course one of the best men of Lion. He has been always fighting for and defending Lion. Whenever he fought, he was reciting:

I am Hawk the son of Sky
chase you away with my sword to protect Lion.
One of two perfect sons,
Lion descends from benevolence and piety.
For Panthera who never lied,
I hit you with ultimate pride.
I wish my soul were divided into two[15].

Fought bravely and fiercely, Hawk killed around 120 people in total until two strong cousins, Mouse and Rat, ambushed and killed him.

When Lion heard about Hawk, he said: "I wish that he had not gone. May God censure those who deserve to be monkeys and pigs."

[15] Maybe, one to fight with Panthera and another with Lion, or he wishes to defend Lion as much as he could.

The Lofty Spirits

MOE JUDY

SCARLET came to Lion, and his servant, Quail, followed him. Scarlet said: "What makes you follow me? What do you want to do?"

Quail said: "What do I want to do? Of course, I want to fight by your side for the sake of Lion until I get killed."

Scarlet said: "This is what I thought. Please, go to Lion so he and I bereave you[16]. This is a day of asking for remuneration from God as much as possible. There is no work after today except for judgment."

Quail came to Lion and said: "Peace be upon you, Lion. May you be under the protection of God." He fought and got killed.

Scarlet came to Lion and said: "Lion, I guarantee that there is no one on earth, close or far, is dearer to me than you. There is nothing more loving to me than defending you. If I had anything dearer than my soul, I would give it

---

[16] In this culture, bereaving a loved one is worse than death.

to you. Peace is upon you. I witness that I follow you and your father's right path."

Unsheathing his sword, Scarlet came to face the army. He was known to have a mark on his forehead. Peccary, one of Swine's knights, saw and recognized Scarlet. Peccary said: "I had seen this man in battles before. He was too brave to be faced with. Hey people, this is the lion of all lions. He is extremely strong. Do not duel with him. Throw him with stones from a distance."

Of course, nobody came to face Scarlet who was saying: "Is not there a man among you to come and fight? Is not there anyone?" Still, nobody wanted to face him. Hog said: "Hit him with stones." The army threw stones at him from all directions. When he saw that, he threw his casque and armor, and charged against the enemy. One of the patrons said: "Are you crazy, Scarlet."

MOE JUDY

Scarlet said: "Yes, and my craze is due to the extreme love of Lion." He charged against the enemy whose men fled away from him.

I had seen him drive away as many as two hundred people. However, the enemy surrounded him from everywhere and finally killed him. His head was found among different men; each of whom claims to have killed him. Hog said: "Do not quarrel amongst yourselves. This man could have never been killed by one person."

The Lofty Spirits

Lion had a servant whose name was Starling who wished to fight for Lion. He started his charge by saying:

The sea boils from my jabs and hits.
The horizon fills up with my arrows.
If my sword is unsheathed,
the heart of the enemy splits.

Starling killed a group of the enemy before he fell. Lion came to and lamented him. Lion put his cheek over Starling's who saw that and smiled before his soul left his body.

MOE JUDY

SWIFT was a servant of one of Panthera's patrons. He also came to support Lion. He fought and when he fell, he called for Lion's help. Lion came and hugged him. Swift said: "Is there anyone like me having his cheek juxtaposed to Lion's." Then, his soul surrendered.

THE LOFTY SPIRITS

EAGLE was always one of the closest patrons of Lion. He was in his fifties. He was charging against the enemy saying: "Get closer, you who killed the faithful people. Get closer, you who killed the sons of Panthera's patrons. Get closer, you who killed the descendants of Panthera and the remaining offspring."

From the other side of the camp, Shrunk told Eagle: "Eagle, how do you see what God has done to you?"

Eagle said: "He did good to me and bad to you."

Shrunk said: "You lied. You never were a liar before. Do you remember when I accompanied you one day, and you said that Hoar was erratic and causing people to go astray and that Panthera was truthful and leading people toward the right path?"

Eagle said: "I witness that this was my opinion and claim."

Shrunk said: "I witness that you are astray."

Eagle said: "Let's fight and let God denounce and terminate the phony."

They fought, and each hit his opponent only once. Shrunk hit first, but his hit did not harm Eagle. However, Eagle hit Shrunk with a lethal strike that Eagle's sword penetrated Shrunk's casque and got stuck in his head. Shrunk fell. Vermin charged against Eagle and wrestled with him for a while. Eagle threw Vermin down and sat on his chest. Vermin cried for help. Weasel charged against Eagle from his behind and jabbed him with a spear. Eagle had to abandon Vermin after biting his nose and cutting it off. One of the men said: "This is the pious Eagle the one who was teaching the holy book in Java." Weasel did not care and killed Eagle with his sword.

It was said that when Weasel came back to his wife, she told him: "You helped kill Lion. You killed the master of the reciters in Java. You have performed a big sin. I swear that I will not talk to you as long as I live."

THE LOFTY SPIRITS

TANAGER was accompanying Lion along with his mother and wife. His mother ordered him: "Get up and fight for the son of Panthera."

He said: "I will do, mother." He did while saying:

If you deny me,
I am the son of a brave father.
You will see me and my hits.
You will hear my charges and attacks.
I will avenge my partners.
I will hide the anguish behind grieves.
My jihad[17] *in battles is not a joke.*

He bravely fought and killed a group of people, and then returned to his wife and mother and said: "Are you satisfied with me, mother?"

---

[17] Jihad has only two forms that are either big (restraining oneself from wrongdoing) and small (defending oneself and family). Some people may claim their offensive attacks to be jihad, but this is totally wrong. They are using the word to cover up for their bad behavior and fool ignorant people.

She said: "No, and I will not until you get killed before Lion." However, his wife entangled with him saying: "Please do not make me bereave you."

His mother said: "Do not listen to her. Go back and fight before the son of Panthera for him to intercede for you during the judgment day."

Tanager returned to the battlefield saying:

I am a leader for you, the mother of Tanager,
while jabbing and hitting.
Hits of a faithful lad for God,
until the enemy tastes the acrimony of war.
I am a man of bitterness and nerve.
I am not a droop during calamity.

While he was charging, he saw his wife holding a shaft saying: "May God sacrifice my parents for you Tanager. Fight for the good people."

He wondered: "Just a while ago, you were thwarting me, and now you are fighting side by side with me."

She said: "Please, do not blame me after hearing Lion."

He said: "What did you hear?"

She said: "I overheard Lion saying while standing by the tent's entrance: 'How few our supporters are!'"

Tanager cried and said: "Get back to the tent, may God bless you."

She refused and said: "I will not get back and wish to die for you."

Tanager asked Lion to coax her back.

Lion told her: "May God bless you, kind household. Get back with the women as they are not supposed to fight."

She went back to the tent. Tanager went back to the field. He fought. Many people surrounded him and cut off his hands, killed and beheaded him; then, they threw his head to Lion's camp. His mother was observing by the door of the tent. She took his head and said: "Congratulations! Going to heaven, Tanager. I ask God that endowed you heaven to accompany me with you."

She took out a pole of a pavilion and charged against the enemy and killed two men of those who killed her son. Lion returned her back to the camp saying: "Get back, mother of Tanager. You and your son are going to heaven with Panthera. Women are not obliged for jihad."

She returned saying: "God does not cut off my hopes."

Lion said: "God will not cut off your hopes, the mother of Tanager."

Tanager's wife walked to his corpse and sat down saying: "Congratulations, darling. I ask God who endowed you heaven to take me with you." Pig told one of his men to beat her head with a shaft, and when he did, she died on top of her husband's chest. She was the first woman to be killed in the battle.

MOE JUDY

TERN was an eleven-year-old boy whose father was a patron of Lion who got already killed. His mother was with him. She told him: "Son, go and fight for Lion." He left the tent. Lion saw him and said: "The father of this youngster already died in the battle. His mother may dislike his leaving the tent." Lion sent him back, but the boy said: "My mother asked me for this, and she already dressed me in my war uniform. Please, allow me to fight to win martyrdom."

Lion took him back to his mother and told her: "Save him. You already lost his father. Let him be."

His mother said: "I hate to see him grow up without his father or you if those thugs let him live, which is something that I cannot guarantee. But I may warrant his triumph and going straight to heaven if he gets killed for your noble cause. Please, let him go. Living under the reign of those people is worthless. If he were left to live, he might end up as a slave and might be treated worse than the Israelis during Ramses' sway. It is either an honorable living or none."

Lion, very well, knew the brutality of the enemy and he saw the mother's point. He reluctantly permitted the boy to go and fight. When the boy went out to the field, he was saying:

My master is Lion, and what a master he is!
He is the cause of happiness in Panthera's heart.
He descends from the best parents ever.
Can you find another match for him?
He has an outset like the sun of dawn.
He has an appearance like a full moon.

Tern fought a fight of heroes. The enemy surrounded him from all over the place, and finally killed him. They threw his head toward Lion's camp. His mother saw the head, took and cleaned it. She said: "Well done son, my source of happiness and pride." She threw back his head to the enemy and hit one of them who instantly died. Then, she took a tent pole wanting to fight while saying:

I am an old and feeble woman.
I am shabby and weak.
I hit you fiercely
for the sake of Lion.

Lion immediately asked her back after he commended her work and he prayed for her.

THE LOFTY SPIRITS

BUNTING wanted to go and fight. He came to ask Lion permission to do so by saying: "Lion, I would like to accompany my dead friends. Also, I hate to stay behind and see you alone."

Lion said: "Go ahead. We will meet soon." Bunting fought until his last breath.

MOE JUDY

THRUSH was always standing in front of Lion to protect him from arrows, spears, swords, and other thrown objects. He was always reciting:

My chest intercepts arrows.
What difference does it make,
throwing an arrow on top of another?
My sword is still in my right hand
like a sea throwing buckets of water.

Thrush yelled: "Hey people, I fear for you what happened to the people of Noah and all infidels who came after. God never wants to oppress people. People, I fear for you the Day of Judgment when you try to flee, but nothing can hide you from the wrath of God. People; do not kill Lion. Only then, God will hurl his resentment over you, and I am not mendacious."

Lion told him: "May God bless you, Thrush. They deserved punishment since the time they rejected the facts that I asked them for when they started to curse you and your companions. Do you think that they will get thwarted after killing your good brothers?"

Thrush said: "That is true, Lion. Should not we go to God and catch up with our brothers?"

Lion said: "Yes, go to what is better than this finite life to an infinite delight."

Thrush said: "Peace be upon you, the son of Panthera. May God rejoin us back in heaven."

Lion replied: "Amen, Amen". Thrush went to the battlefield. He fought courageously until he was outnumbered and killed.

MOE JUDY

TWO youthful brothers, Dove and Pigeon, came to Lion and said: "Lion, peace be upon you. We came here to protect you and get killed for you."

Lion said: "Welcome! Come closer." They closed in and they were crying. Lion said: "Why and what are you crying for? It is just a matter of a short time, and you will be much happier."

They said: "We are not lamenting ourselves, but you we are crying because we see you surrounded by ruthless beasts, and we can neither be of good to you nor we can protect you from any harm."

Lion said: "May God endow you with the best reward. Your support and sacrifice are the best that one can receive." They stated their farewell to Lion. They fought and got killed.

KITE was a good archer. He soaked lots of his arrows in poison and used them to throw at the enemy. Kite wrote his name on each of these arrows. For this he was saying:

I throw marked arrows,
poisoned to inflect sorrows.

When his arrows depleted, he unsheathed his sword and improvised:

I am a person from Ora.
My religion is the one
for Lion and Panthera.
If I get killed today,
I get a wish granted.
This is my belief,
when I face God with relief.

He killed twelve people and injured many more. The enemy surrounded him while throwing stones, blades, and spearheads. They broke his upper arms. They captured and took him to Pig who took him to Hog. Hog said: "Woe on you Kite. What have you done to yourself? What made you do such a foolish thing?"

While blood was flowing on his face and beard, Kite replied: "Only God knows what I wanted."

After seeing the hemorrhage, a man told Kite: "Don't you see what has happened to you?"

Kite said: "I killed twelve of your men. I injured many others. I do not blame myself for being toiled. If I had not lost my arms, you would not be able to capture me."

Pig unsheathed his sword to kill Kite who said: "I swear that if you were a righteous person, you would revise yourself for killing decent people. Thank God who chose our death at the hands of bad people." Pig decapitated him.

THE LOFTY SPIRITS

AN old black servant of Lion, John, wanted to fight. Lion told him: "You accompanied us to eke out a living. Therefore, you are free to go now. Do not get afflicted with our affairs."

John replied: "The son of Panthera. At ease, I lick your plate, and you want me to abscond when you are at stake! I know that I smell. I do not come from an honorable ancestry. My color is too dark. I need to feel the breeze of heaven so that my bad smell goes away, I become dignified, and my face turns white[18]. I swear that I am not leaving until my black blood blends with yours."[19] Lion granted his wish and permitted him to fight. While John was fighting, he improvised:

How do infidels see the hits of a lion?
Hits to defend the family of Lion.

[18] This is a figure of speech that should not be taken literary. As explained before, white means good and black means; it has nothing to do with the skin color.

[19] A figure of speech and since there is no blue blood, there is no black one. Blood is only red.

Moe Judy

My tongue and hand protect them
in hope to get to heaven, then.

He fought until he was killed. Lion stood by his corpse and said: "God. Please, whiten[20] his face, sweeten his smell, and group him with the good people."

---

[20] This is a figure of speech. People usually use white for good and black for bad, such as black magic. This may be a misnomer as there should be no difference among people due to their different color of skin. Being good or bad has nothing to do with the race.

THE LOFTY SPIRITS

TOWHEE was a very old man who fought along with Panthera in his wars against the infidels who enslaved people and abducted wives from their husbands. Strapping his back and holding his eyebrows with a swathe, he came to Lion to ask for permission to fight. When Lion saw him like this, he cried and said: "Thank you, old man." Although he was very old and barely able to hold his body parts without the support of artificial garments, he managed to kill eighteen people before getting killed. It was faith and not the body that was fighting. Fighting for the love of life is different from fighting for the love of God. People who fight for temporal prosperity will not fight as those who do not care if they die and look forward to perpetuity.

MOE JUDY

THIS was what happened. A man came after another to ask Lion for permission to fight. Everyone strode toward the field as if he were being sent to his bride at a wedding night. They were truly loyal and faithful. They fought to the last man, concluding strength and the last drop of blood until all patrons were gone.

The Lofty Spirits

Lion was left only with seventeen of his relatives to face that ruthless army. Lion was left with some of his sons, brothers from different mothers, nephews, and cousins. They all gathered to farewell each other.

On the previous night, Lion asked everyone to leave except for his son Leopard and brother Tiger. He said that these two were his army.

Lion loved Leopard more than anything in life. He adored him for many reasons. At twenty-five, Leopard was thought to be the most handsome and noble person at that time to the point that poets wrote many poems for him, one of which was

No eye had seen one like him,
neither with nor without shoes.
I mean the son of Lion,
I mean the son of Leela.
He does not prefer life over his religion.
He does not sell the good for bad.

Moe Judy

With his ethics, out of the relatives, Lion did not want to send anyone to the field before Leopard. Leopard came to his father to ask for permission. Despondent, Lion looked at him, cried, and raised his two forefingers to the sky and said: "God, witness that these people are killing the only person in this life who looks like Panthera in appearance, religiosity, manners, ethics, and verbatim. Whenever we wished to commemorate Panthera, we looked at him. O God, stop rain from falling, divide them, shatter them, make every one of them go a separate way, and never please any ruler with them. They summoned us for support but turned against us to kill."

Lion yelled at Hog: "As you cut off mine, may God cut off your kinship and his benediction. May He send someone to slay you on your bed."

Leopard went to the battlefield while improvising:

I am Leopard,
the son of Lion.

We are worthier
to earn the reign of Panthera.
Never will Swine rule us.
My sword hits to defend my father
and hits like the Felidaes[21].

When my brother appeared to the enemy, all men were terrified. For instance, it appeared that Panthera rose back to espouse his beloved son, Lion. It was well known that nobody could ever face Panthera, the bravest and strongest man ever born, for it meant destined bereavement.

Hog's face turned yellow, and his throat dried out. None of his men wanted to face Leopard or wanted to be in front of the army. Pig suggested that Hyena, the bravest and strongest man Hog had, confront Leopard.

---

[21] It is well known that the Felidaes have the strongest hits. During wars, Panthera used to cut the people of the enemy into two halves: either vertically or horizontally.

Lion was watching from a distance and his facial looks changed when he saw the other duelist. Leopard's mother, Leela, was watching Lion's face from inside her tent. She sensed the danger, and she approached Lion, hurriedly. She wondered if anything wrong happened to her son. Lion assured her not, but Leopard was facing a valiant and tough rival. Lion asked her to go back to the tent and pray for Leopard, and she did.

Hyena stood firmly and said: "I hate to waste a young man like you." Leopard replied: "But I want you to do so. I will be eager to combat you." Hyena lost his temper and started to attack.

As they were fighting, Lion's face was variegating. Leela was watching him and holding her breath. After a very long fight, swiftly, Leopard opened his arm as far as he could. Horizontally, he struck Hyena very hard. Hyena did not feel the hit and as he started to move on his horse, he was split into two halves (i.e., upper and lower). As Leela kept watching, Lion's face flashed up. She knew that Leopard dispatched Hyena.

Hog was pest off and ordered many of his men to attack at once. None of them returned safely. He resumed the order more than once, but the same conclusion persisted.

Leopard was fighting fiercely until the enemy fed up with the number of their casualties. Leopard was overpowered by fatigue and thirst; therefore, he returned to Lion for a short rest. Leopard said to Lion: "Kings hunt foxes and rabbits, but I hunt heroes and I want my reward." "What reward do you want son?" Lion replied. "I want a sip of water," Leopard stated. He told Lion: "Father, thirst has killed me. The weight of steel has strained me."

A moment of silence and staring took place. Lion said: "I wish I had some to give. Why don't you try to wit your mouth with the moist of mine?" Lion stung his tongue out and it was as stiff as a piece of wood. Leopard felt ashamed of himself to ask his father for such a wish.

Lion said: "Fight a little more and soon you will meet your grandpa and he will quench you with his Fuller Glass that you will never feel thirst after."

Lion told his son to visit his mother in her tent. Leopard did and found his mother unconscious. He put her head on his lap trying to get her up. His tears came down her face and she awakened. She said, "My dear son, is this a dream?" He said "No." She hugged and sniffed him. He wanted to leave, but she was grabbing him very tightly. She asked him to walk in front of her; back and forth. After sorrowful moments, he asked her for permission to leave. She could not tell him "yes" or "no" because she was shocked. Grudgingly, he left the tent. His mother improvised:

Oh,
my son,

I love you
as much as "love" has been said.
I love you
as much as "love" has been written.
I love your sun.
I love your shade.
I love my days
when you are there.
I love your talks.
I love your silence.
I love being cheerful or troubled for you.
I love the night
because you are the moon and its luminosity.
I love light
because you are the glow of this life.
If I do not see you for one day,
I perceive your loom in mind.
I wonder if you know that
my life and control
are at your wish.
I will sing and repeat for you
until the last moment of my time:

MOE JUDY

I love you.
I love you,
more than anything in life.

It did not take long until Leopard went back to the field of battle. In the meanwhile, Hog realigned his men and ordered some of them to pull Leopard toward the army camp and never give him a chance to retreat. The farther they took him away from his father's camp, the easier they could circle and, hence, defeat him.

Leopard went back to the field charging many times against the enemy while saying:

The war has shown facts.
The truth has been released.
I swear, we will never flee
away from you
until all our flags go down.

As the combat resumed, Leopard killed and injured many of them as expected, but countless fighters surrounded him like killer ants surrounding a live prey to eat its flesh alive with their mandibles.

Wolverine looked at him from a distance and said: "I deserve all the sins and shame of the nation if he comes nearby, and I do not bereave his parents."

Zipping through the crowd on a racing horse with a speed of an eagle, Wolverine came from Leopard's behind and gored him with a long spear whose impact knocked him over the neck of his horse. His casque came off and almost fainted. Hoping to get back to Lion's camp, he tightly held to the horse's neck when he lost his sword. Wolverine again hit him on his head with his sword. Moreover, the battalions started to hit him with their armory wherever possible from all directions.

The blood started to seep from his forehead and blocked the horse's eyes. The horse panicked and fled toward the enemy's camp. Every scalawag hit him until he was completely butchered. His pieces fell apart all over the place until there was nothing to save out of him.

When Leopard felt that he was dying, he yelled: "Farewell, dad. Here is my grandpa who offered me my glass of water. I do not feel thirsty anymore. He says that there is a glass saved for you."

Lion heard the drums of victory coming out from the enemy's camps. He knew that his son was finished. Lamented, he rode his horse and sped up like a cheetah chasing prey.

Lion charged toward his son. Everyone from the enemy fled. Lion fell over Leopard. Put his cheek over Leopard's and said: "May God abolish people who killed you. How could they do it in front of God? How daring they are! Life is worthless after you, son. It is really hard for your grandpa and father that you summon but cannot help you." He put his son on his lap and wailed for a while until his beard turned white[22].

Lion asked the remaining relatives to carry Leopard to the main pavilion. He asked them to bring a blanket to collect Leopard's parts in. The pieces of Leopard were carried to the tent while kids and women were watching. When my aunt Lioness saw this, she threw herself on Leopard's body while crying: "O my God. O Panthera. O Leopard."

Leela went crazy when she saw her son slain this way. She did not know what to do. One time she kissed him. Another, she got a whiff out of him. Inconsolable, she finally lay down next to him. She improvised:

Son,
where are you?
The light of my heart,
where are you?

[22] Analysts and historians believe that Lion dyed his beard, and his tears wore off the black color.

Moe Judy

The radiance of my soul,
where are you?
O my God,
where are you?
Bewildered,
I wish to see you one more time
to light up my life
and fill it with your intensity.
I hug you with my soul,
and heal my wounds.
My essence,
what is my fault
when I loved you?
There was nothing
I did not give you
for love.
I spent nights
holding your spirit.
In my life,
you are my fate and destiny.
Please, do not leave me alone.
I swear I have no one else.

The Lofty Spirits

ANGORA[23], another young man and a cousin of Lion, went next to the field while improvising:

Today I meet my father,
and the other lads
who were killed
holding the right belief.
They are not people of lies,
but of honor and lineage.
They are from those masters,
the Felidaes.

Three times he charged against the enemy before Maggot threw an arrow at him. Angora wanted to protect his face with his hand from the shooting arrow; however, the arrow nailed his palm to his forehead. He tried to remove the arrow and free his hand, but he could not. Then, he said: "God, they murdered us because we are few. Please, terminate them for assassinating us." As he was

[23] His father was a cousin of Lion who sent him to Java as a messenger, but he was captured and decapitated.

baffled, another rascal jabbed him in his heart and Angora died instantly.

MOE JUDY

WHEN Angora died, his uncles, brothers, and cousins all charged at once. Lion told them: "Forbearance, cousins. Death is soon; however, after that, you will not meet humiliation or oppression."

They all fought bravely and indubitably died because they were outnumbered, of course.

THE LOFTY SPIRITS

AFTER all the cousins, Lion was left only with a few of his brave brothers, including Tiger, of course. Lion did not want Tiger to leave the campsite. His presence there thwarted the bravest men of the enemy from approaching and terrorizing the kids and women. After all, Tiger was matchless.

A thirteen-year-old nephew of Lion, Margay, came to Lion to ask him to face the enemy. Lion loved this boy since the day he raised him as an orphan. Lion hugged him. Both cried until they fainted. Margay wanted permission, but Lion declined. Margay continuously kissed Lion's hands for acquiescence. Lion finally allowed him to do so. He was happy to get Lion's consent. He went to the battlefield and his tears were coming down his cheeks. He was improvising:

If they denied me,
I am the son of Ocelot,
the son of faithful Panthera.
Here is Lion like a prisoner,

Moe Judy

among rascals and thugs.

Although he was very young that barely reached puberty, he fought intrepidly and killed several men of the enemy.

The historian and narrator of the enemy, Worm, said: "A boy came out of Lion's camp. His face was like a full moon. His sword was unsheathed and held by his right hand. He wore a shirt and a loincloth. He wore a pair of sandals. A thong of his sandal broke, and I remember it to be the left one. He knelt to fix it overlooking the thousands of men surrounding him, during which Parasite came charging against him. I [Worm] told him: 'what do you want from the boy? Don't you see those surrounding him already?' Parasite said: 'To kill him.' Yes, he did by hitting him on the head. Margay fell on his face. Bewildered, his mother was looking from her tent."

When my cousin, Margay, fell, he cried: "O Uncle."

My father, Lion, came like a charging lion, and with his sword, he hit Parasite who intercept Lion's sword with his arm that he instantly lost. Parasite squalled loudly and was heard by his camp whose people came to help him. Unfortunately for him, the many horses came to rescue him, stepped over, and killed him.

When the dust cleared, Lion was seen near Margay while he was jolting the ground with his two legs. Lion said: "Woe on people who killed you. Their adversaries will be your father and grandfather during judgment day. Sadly, you summoned your uncle, but he could not answer duly. When he answered, it was too late."

Chest by chest, Lion lifted Margay whose feet were touching the ground[24]. He placed him near Leopard and the other bodies. Lion said: "God, tally all the guilty people, kill them when they are separated, do not leave out any of them, and do not absolve them no matter what."

---

[24] It was believed that either the boy was tall or that Lion was too heartbroken to stay upright.

Moe Judy

THE LOFTY SPIRITS

LION was left on the battlefield with seven brothers from three different mothers. Along with Lion, these are all the remaining sons of Panthera[25]. All these brothers were younger than Lion. Tiger came second after Lion, and he was only 34. The rest were younger than Tiger, and the youngest was 21.

Birman came first to ask Lion's permission. He came to the battlefield improvising:

My old man is Panthera,
who deserves the highest praise.
He is from the noble Felidaes.
This is Lion,
the son of Acinonyx[26].

---

[25] One of, yet from another mother, was left in Bourg because he had leprosy.

[26] Lion's mother is thought to be the most venerated women whose father was a great well-respected king. Birman here proves that Lion's mother was more honourable than his. All Lion's brothers faithfully believed that his mother is better than theirs because she was chosen by God. Therefore, they held all the respect for him along with their belief of him to be the legitimate heir of Panthera.

For him,
we fight with our swords.
I sacrifice myself,
for a venerated brother.

Especially with the frantic army[27] who wants to finish the deal, it did not take long to terminate Birman who was killed by Nematoda.

Birman's full brother, Burmilla came next and followed Nematoda to kill him while he was saying:

I hit you all
but I do not see Nematoda,
that rascal who became an infidel.
Nematoda, O Nematoda,
come closer to Burmilla
as you may end up in hell.

---

[27] They changed their tactics. Now they attack all at once instead of dueling since they realized that they could not do it anymore with courageous knights who are fighting to die.

Burmilla managed to kill Nematoda and then he went forward to meet the army while reciting:

Leave me alone,
the enemy of God.
Leave the charging lion alone.
Not retreating,
he bravely hits you with his sword.
He is not a hiding coward.

After a great battle, Burmilla was finally terminated.

MOE JUDY

THEN, Caracal came out. An arrow hit him. He was killed and decapitated.

THE LOFTY SPIRITS

WHEN Tiger saw three half-brothers already killed, he asked three of his full brothers, Cymric, Kodkod, and Korat to combat the enemy: "The sons of my mother, go forward until I see you do your best to defend Lion. Make me proud."

Cymric was 25. He entered the battlefield while saying:

I am the son of the rescuer
kind Panthera the doer,
the sword of God,
the bitter.

Cymric fought Annelida, who killed him.

Cymric's younger brother, Kodkod, who was 23 came next saying:

I am Kodkod,
the majestic,
the son of Panthera,
the imperial.

Moe Judy

I inherited great honor
from both sides of uncles.

Kodkod was killed by Annelida, who decapitated him.

Korat, 21, came after both of his brothers saying:

I am Korat,
the regal,
the son of Panthera,
the royal.
My brother Lion
is the best of the best.
He is the master of
old and young people,
after Panthera who was never feeble.

Korat was hit from a distance by an arrow; then, killed and decapitated.

THE LOFTY SPIRITS

ONLY Tiger was left with Lion who wanted to spare him to defend the camp. The death of Tiger meant a total collapse. Whenever Lion went to the field, he made sure that Tiger was behind. Otherwise, Lion would send Tiger and stay behind.

Among many good attributes and good nicknames, Tiger was dubbed the "water man" because he always brought water to the camp after the siege. He was also called the "full moon" of the Felidaes because he was very handsome, and his face was luminous. He was tall, well-built, and muscular. Whenever he rode a horse, his feet approached the ground. Lion gave him the banner of the camp since he was the strongest and most reliable.

Tiger, who always wore a distinctive panache on his casque, came to take permission from Lion who said: "Tiger, you are the holder of my banner."

Tiger said: "My chest has become tight. I am fed up with life. I need to take my revenge on those hypocrites."

Lion told him: "Before going to the battle, can you ask for some water for the kids."

Tiger went to the army, preached and warned them, and said: "Hog, this is Lion the son of Acinonyx. You killed his patrons and relatives. Only his youngsters remained, and they are thirsty. Can we get them some water as thirst flamed their hearts?”

Pig replied: "Tiger, if the whole face of the earth were covered with fresh water and it was under our control, we would not give you a drop until you succumb to Swine."

Tiger went back to Lion to tell him what happened. Tiger heard the kids say: "Thirst, thirst." He rode his horse and took the big canteen that was made of animal skin. He wanted to reach Forbearance which was around 600 meters[28] away from Lion's camp and four thousand people secured the gap. When he was charging to the water, the enemy

[28] Around 2000 feet.

hurled so many arrows that covered the sky above him, but he neither cared for their weapons nor their number.

He managed to clear his way to the water. He came down to drink. He was so thirsty that his stomach was burning like a furnace. He took some water with his palms; nevertheless, he remembered the thirst of Lion and his family. Therefore, he threw the water and said:

Hey self,
hold your horses.
You need to calm down.
You are naught before Lion,
and nothing after him.
He is Lion,
who is drinking hot death,
and you are drinking cold water.
I swear that this is not
my religiosity doing
that suits my certitude.

Extremely parched, Tiger filled up the canteen and headed back toward the camp. The enemy surrounded him from every direction; nevertheless, he was charging and saying:

I do not care if death comes.
I am Tiger taking the water.
I sacrifice myself for Lion.

He penetrated and diffused them. Nobody, I mean nobody, was able to hold a position in front of him. When Tiger charged, he paved the way behind him.

Hog was watching. He yelled: "You fools will never be able to get him down when you are surrounding him as our archers cannot reach him. Moreover, if he delivered the water to the camp, between him and Lion, you would become easy prey for them. You idiots cannot take him down when he is thirsty. Can you imagine how he would be if he drank some water?"

The men scattered, and Tiger was ambushed. Sipuncula hid behind a palm tree and hit Tiger on his right arm, and it was cut from the elbow. Tiger took the sword by his left hand without fear or despair, as his mission was to deliver the water to the camp while saying:

If you cut off my right arm,
I infinitely defend my faith
and a truthful leader,
the son of Panthera.

This time Priapulida ambushed him behind a different tree and cut off Tiger's left arm. Then, he hugged the banner and said:

O self,
never fear the infidels,
and just wait for His mercy,
when you join Panthera.
God, they cut off my left arm.
Burn them in hell.

This was when they started to launch numerous arrows that came at him like a shower. One of the arrows pierced the canteen and the water drained out. This is the moment when Tiger got downhearted. He stood at the spot when many other arrows showered him.

One of the arrows landed on his chest and another one from Boar on his right eye. Then, he bowed down to remove the arrow from his eye with his knees; however, a rascal hit him with a shaft from steel on his head. Tiger fell, and shouted: "Peace be upon you, Lion."

Lion came and found Tiger in pieces. Tiger could not see because one of his eyes was lost and the other had blood blobs built above it. When Tiger heard someone near him, he said: "Hey, you. I ask you by whom you worship to spare me until Lion comes. I am not afraid to die, but I want to make sure that Lion is safe before I die."

Sobbing, Lion replied: "I am your brother, Lion. Now, my back has been broken. Now, I do not know what to do. Now, the enemy gloats over my grief."

Lion sat down and took Tiger's head to clean it. Lion put Tiger's head in his lap, but Tiger jerked it off. Another time, Lion put Tiger's head in his lap, but Tiger still jerked it off. Lion said: "Why do every time I put your head in my lap you yank it off?" Tiger said: "Who will put your head in his lap when you fall?"

Lion wanted to carry down Tiger to the camp, but Tiger refused to go. Lion wondered why. Tiger said: "I feel ashamed to go back without water. They all have hopes for me. Please, leave me here."

Weeping, Lion started to clean off Tiger's head when he passed away. At that time, Lion charged like an eagle and the enemy fled like prey. Lion was saying to them: "Where are you fleeing to when you murdered my brother? Where are you escaping to when you killed my right arm?"

Moe Judy

Broken and sad, Lion returned to the camp weeping and wiping away his tears with his sleeves. Hopeful, his daughter Cheetah came and asked him about Tiger. He went to Tiger's tent and broke its pole. When Lioness saw this, she came out and cried: "O brother. O, Tiger. We are lost after you." Along with Lion, all the women and kids cried, and Lion said: "Yes, we are lost without you, Tiger."

The Lofty Spirits

LION lost all the men around him. He looked right and left but did not see anyone who could fight for him. He looked at his patrons and relatives, and they were all butchered. During all of this, the weeping and crying of the kids and women were filling up his ears. Lion shouted: "Is there anyone willing to defend our women? Is there a theist who fears God? Is there a champion who wishes for God's salvation? Is there a supporter who wishes God's reward?" The weeping and sobbing elevated.

MOE JUDY

LION went to Lioness by the door of the tent and asked her to bring him his youngest son, Kitten, who was only 6 months. Lion wanted to farewell the child. When Kitten was brought, Lion put him in his lap and saw him panting due to thirst.

Lion took the child with him to the enemy camp and said: "This is an infant. If he lived, he would not fight against you. If he died, you would be asked for his blood. Please, give him some water. If you are afraid that I take the water for me, take him and give him some drinks, and then bring him back."

The enemy site split into two camps: one to give water to the child and another that opposed this idea. The two camps argued. Hog told Boar, the specialist archer, to cut off the dispute. Boar asked: "Do you want me to give him water?" Hog said: "No, reward him with one of your arrows."

In the beginning, Boar did not know where to hit the child, but he saw Kitten's neck that was shining like silverware. He put one of his special arrows into his bow and launched it toward the child. The arrow penetrated Kitten's neck. Feeling the pain, Kitten took out his arm from his cotton cover. It did not take Kitten long to pass away, but this for sure affected Lion's spirit, dramatically.

Lion collected some of Kitten's blood and threw it to the sky while saying: "The only thing that eases this is that it is done while God is observing everything. God, if you held away victory from us, please reward us with something better. God, retaliate against the oppressors. God, accumulate our current perils to reward us with something better when needed. God, you are the witness of people killing every soul we have."

Lion dug a grave with his sword and buried Kitten.

MOE JUDY

UNSHEATHING Panthera's sword, Lion came to the enemy wearing his father's war attire. He told the enemy: "I am a single person, and you are thousands. Let's make duels."

Lion managed to kill everyone who came to combat him. Hog said: "Are you fools? Do you know whom you are fighting? Being the son of Panthera is enough. I swear that if all of you combated him one by one, he would terminate you all. Besides, we cannot take advantage of our numbers."

Hearing this, Lion charged against the right-wing while saying:

Death is worthier than shame.
Shame is superior to hell.

Everyone fled. Then, he charged against the left wing while saying:

I am Lion the son of Panthera.

THE LOFTY SPIRITS

I vow not to bow.
I protect my family.
I die with the creed of Panthera.

Worm said: "O my God. I have not seen someone whose sons, brothers, and patrons died more imperturbable than Lion. I have not encountered anyone more intrepid. I swear that I neither saw before nor after one like him. Men surrounded him from all angles, and when he charged, they fled away like prey escaping a predator. They were around thirty thousand leaping away from him like grasshoppers. He did that and managed to go back to his center every time while lauding God."

When Pig saw this, he called all the knights and placed them at the back of infantries. He ordered the archers to shower Lion. When they did, Lion's armor became like a porcupine. Then, Pig and some of his men separated Lion from his camp. Lion yelled: "Woe on you. If you do not have any religion and you do not fear the Day of Judgment, be freeborn and revise your calculations if you are of dignity."

Pig said: "What do you say, the son of Acinonyx?"

Lion said: "I say that I am fighting you. It is neither the women nor the kids. Keep your ferocity away from my family as long as I live."

Pig said: "You got this, Lion." Then he yelled at his men to stay away from Lion's family and direct their efforts only against him. They charged against him, but he managed to scatter them. He was extremely thirsty and tough.

Consequently, he headed to Forbearance to get some water. There were four thousand people, but he managed to penetrate them and reach the river. He entered the water riding his horse. When the mare felt the water, she lowered her head to drink. Lion said: "You are thirsty, and I am as well. I swear that I will not drink until you do so." As if she understood what Lion said, the mare refused to drink and raised her head. When Lion took some water in his palm, the army shouted: "You drink water when your family was attacked." Lion threw the water and headed back to the camp.

When he reached the camp, he found it intact. He knew that it was a trick to thwart him from drinking.

This time, Lion asked all his family to get out of the tents for the last farewell. He asked them to get patient and wear as many clothes as they could and said: "Be ready for peril. Know that God is protecting and saving you from these people. You will end up fine, but they will not. He is going to punish them badly. He is going to compensate you with many other good things. Do not complain or say anything that might debase your values."

As he was preaching to the family, he looked at his daughter Cheetah who was busy with her piety. He saw her taking a side and crying. He stood by her and said:

Moe Judy

This is the final farewell.
Our next meeting is on judgment day.
Leave crying behind.
Get ready to get apprehended.
Be more patient when
you see me bleeding from everywhere
on sand.

When Hog saw Lion busy with his family, Hog said: "Attack him, you fools. It is our only chance to assault him when he is busy. I swear that if he concentrated on fighting you, you would not know your rights from lefts."

They attacked him, and the archers threw thousands of arrows at him and his camp. The family got startled. The women and kids got frightened, cried, and entered the tents looking at Lion to see what he would do.

Lion charged against the enemy. Everyone he followed fell dead. The arrows come to him from all directions. They mainly hit his chest and neck.

The Lofty Spirits

He returned to his center while lauding God. He looked parched. Pig said: "You will not taste water until you get to hell. Do not you see Forbearance like snake bottoms? You will not drink and will die thirsty."

He continued fighting. He accumulated 72 wounds. He said: "God, you see how my condition is due to the defiance of these rascals. God, tally them all and kill them one by one. Do not leave anyone from them on earth. Do not ever forgive them."

Lion yelled at the enemy: "Hey, the nation of sins. Woe on you for the way you have treated Panthera's offspring. After me, you will not have a second thought about killing innocent people; anytime, it will be too easy for you to kill anyone. I hope that God endows me martyrdom and chastises you when you least expect it."

MOE JUDY

WITH farfetched thirst and fatigue, Lion finally stopped to rest. Nemertea threw a stone that hit Lion's forehead. The blood came down on his face and beard. Lion took his shirt to wipe out the blood. Boar saw the whiteness of Lion's abdomen and threw a poisoned arrow that was made specially to hit Lion. The arrowhead was three-dimensional; namely, like a three-faced prism.

Lion tried to take out the arrow from the front, but he could not. Accordingly, he pressed against the horn of the saddle to get the arrow from his back. He managed to get it but with two-thirds of his liver. The blood came out like water coming out of a gutter during heavy rain. Hence, he fell from his mare. As he hit the ground, he said: "In the name of God and the faith of Panthera."

He raised his head to the heavens and said: "God, you know that they are killing the last son of Acinonyx."

He took some of his blood and threw it toward the sky and said: "God, I complain to you about what is being done to the son of Acinonyx."

Bleeding and exhausted, Lion sat on the ground when Hemichordata cussed him and hit his head. The burnoose[29] Lion was wearing got filled with blood. Lion told Hemichordata: "You may not eat or drink with your hands again. May God group you with oppressors during the judgment day." Lion threw out his burnoose.

---

[29] A one-piece hooded cloak worn by Arabs and Berbers.

MOE JUDY

WHILE Lion was in this condition, an 11-year-old nephew, Lynx, came to him after escaping from Lioness, who tried to thwart him, but she could not. Lion was not able to get up and was surrounded by a merciless enemy. Lynx stood by his uncle, during which Nematomorpha hit Lion with his sword when Lynx intercepted it and lost his right arm. He said to Lion: "Uncle, they have cut off my arm." Lion hugged him and said: "My nephew, be patient and know that God's rewards are much worthier." Boar threw an arrow and killed the boy.

Lion was situated down on the ground for a while. If the enemy had wished to kill him, they could have done so except that each tribe wanted to evade killing him and wanted another tribe to attempt this furthermost sin and embarrassment.

Cestoda recorded: "I was standing with Hog's men when someone shouted: 'Be happy my master. There is Pig wanting to kill Lion.' I went out to witness the incident. I saw Lion busy with his agonies. I swear that I have not seen a victim covered with blood that had a more glowing face than Lion's whose luminosity distracted me from trying to kill him. Lion looked extremely dehydrated. A man told him: 'You will not taste water until you get to hell.' Lion replied: 'I go to hell and drink its boiling water! No, I swear. I will go to my father and meet him in heaven and live with him in his palace. Then, I will complain about you all.'"

They all got upset to the point that as if God did not leave any kindness in their black hearts.

Pig shouted: "Woe on you idiots. What are you waiting for? Don't you see that the man cannot even stand? Attack him, may your mothers bereave you." Many charged against him from all directions. Chaetognatha hit Lion on his shoulder strongly. Lion fell on his face. Lion cycled between getting up and falling. Onychophora jabbed Lion in his clavicle and ribs. Dung threw Lion an arrow that hit his neck. Feces jabbed Lion in his flank. Lion fell. He sat and took out the arrow from his neck.

Moe Judy

Lion was receiving his blood from his two palms and whenever they filled, he dyed his head and beard with his blood. Lion said: "This is how I meet God, dyed with my own blood."

THE LOFTY SPIRITS

LION'S mare started to go in circles and bedaubed her forehead with Lion's blood. Then, she went to the camp while neighing loudly, the neigh of a genuine horse that lost its knight. When the women looked at the horse having many arrows piercing its body and the saddle was contorted, they took off from the camp, weeping while slapping their faces, to Lion's body.

One of them with sympathy
hugs him.
A second with her cloths
provides shade.
A third with his blood
dyes her face.
A fourth protects,
and a fifth kisses.
A sixth, with fear,
resort to him.
Another one,
from what happened,
lost grasp.

MOE JUDY

Lioness cried: "O my God. O, my father. O Panthera. Here is Lion knocked down in Coccus. I wish that the sky fell on earth and mountains crushed down."

When she got closer to Lion and Hog was nearby with some of his men, while Lion was suffering, she said: "Hog, will Lion get killed and you are watching?" Bashfully, Hog averted his face away from her.

She continued: "Woe on you all. Is not there a decent man among you?" Nobody answered.

HOG yelled at his men: "Get down and take care of him." Pig came down and kicked him. Lion fell. Pig sat down on Lion's chest with his iron boots. Lion said: "Panthera was right when he told me that someone who looks like dogs and pigs would kill me." Pig fumed, but he could not kill Lion while looking at his face. He flipped Lion over. He held Lion's beard. He hit Lion's neck twelve times until he separated the head from the body. Pig stuck the head on a spear top.

MOE JUDY

THE thugs surrounded Lion's body to rob him. Someone looted his shirt. Another pillaged his turban. Another despoiled his sandals. Another stole his pants. The last person to come found nothing to snatch except for a ring stained with blood on his pinky finger. He cut off his finger to steal the ring. Then, the thugs brawled amongst themselves for dividing the plunder.

WHILE telling the story, Jaguar stopped many times to weep or cry. When he reached this part, he fainted. Many listeners cried as well, some of whom even wept.

After recovery, he was asked: "What happened next? How did you come out of it?" He said: "This was another long story that may need to be told at another time."

Before departure, Jaguar improvised:

I cry about our calamitous fait accompli,
and endure torture and desolation tragedy.
Sad, I stood
staring at the hungry faces
and loaf of bread.

Moe Judy

I read mishaps and their episodes
over the veracious look.
I hid tears on my eyeball,
but grief showed on the rip bents.
I hovered over a sanguineous horizon,
knocked down and
shrouded with tears.
Hey, night!
What does dark conceal?
Does it bear hatred until sunshine?
And does my era veil the tissue of blood
for millions of deprived people, quietly?
Hey fair adjudicator?
Where is protection?
They are like wolves
and we are the herd.
We want a decent life,
but they want a fast demise.
Nevertheless,
If I had to be tormented,
My neck would be a sword,
and my blood hemorrhage.

REFERENCES

Michael Pollard (2005). *THE COMPLETE ENCYCLOPEDIA OF CATS.* UK: Parragon Publishing.

Brian Richard (2006). *A Field Guide to the WILDLIFE of North America.* UK: Atlantic Publishing.

Michael Vanner (2007). *A Field Guide to the BIRDS of North America.* UK: Parragon Publishing.

Mohammad Huwaidi (aka Moe Judy) was born in the winter of 1965. He grew up with a love of mathematics. He received many best student awards during his schooling. After graduating from high school, he was granted a scholarship sponsored by Aramco. In 1989, he graduated from the University of Tulsa with Computer Science and Applied Math. He earned his master's degree in Computer Science and Software Engineering from KFUPM in 1997. He joined the University of Colorado at Boulder for a Ph.D. program (2010). Then he transferred to Aspen University in Denver. He conducted many critical-technical projects in Saudi Aramco that revolutionized the company's computer center and capabilities as he partook a leading role in building the largest supercomputer in the Middle East and Europe in 2001. In 2003, he earned a US-Patent. He retired from Saudi Aramco in the summer of 2004. He currently works as an independent HPC specialist. His specialties include algorithms, optimization, parallel & distributed applications, and high-performance computing. He published an allegory, *Saved by Simple Logic*, multiple technical papers, hundreds of articles, and several books in Arabic. He married Hoda Selham in 1987, having three children: Mustafa (1989), Murtadha (1991), and Mujtaba (1993).

The Lofty Spirits is heartbreaking when thousands of soldiers attacked around 100 people who were butchered and maimed. The reader may get sentimental due to the brutality of the assailing army and the gory fate of the victims, and it is fine to do so; the author himself cried whenever writing and reviewing. Being empathetic is good for expressing feelings, cleansing the soul, and expelling the toxins out of the body. This may be a heck of a ride; hold your stomach tight.

www.ingramcontent.com/pod-product-compliance
Lightning Source LLC
LaVergne TN
LVHW060838170826
845678LV00007B/1800

* 9 7 9 8 3 7 3 9 6 7 4 6 4 *